This book is dedicated to my Mother Susan Pike, who has always taken great care of me and has loved me unconditionally even in the worst of times. I love you Mom.

A special thanks to Ellen Degeneres, who's kindness and unselfishness has made me want to become the best I can be. This book was my first step in making my life and others better. You give people hope, keep up the good work.

To my Editor Traci Long, thank you for all your hard work.

PROLOGUE

The first thing Rookie John Stark of the San Diego Sheriffs department thought when he saw the two naked bodies, half behind some overgrown bushes, and just behind the corner of a cement structure concealing a garbage dumpster, was that he stumbled upon two lovers just trying to have some fun.

"Funs over guys, put your clothes on and get out of here."

No response, and with no movement Stark stepped closer and drew his flashlight.

What he saw he knew would haunt him the rest of his life. Two naked teenage girls lay side by side. One with long blonde hair, slim and very pretty in the face. The other girl had short black hair, cut just below her ears. He guessed she might weigh about a hundred and ten pounds, but could not tell if her face had ever been pretty. They looked dead to him, real dead. He

William Pike

shined his flashlight back over to the blonde girl as he started to yell for his partner.

"Bob!"

Bob was still inside the gas station buying a couple red bulls, and whatever else might help keep them awake all night. Then Deputy Stark remembered his radio.

"This is 2110, I have a possible double homicide, at the corner of Pepper street and Winter Gardens behind that thrifty gas station. Please send back up and an EMT."

"2110 that's a copy, backup is in route" was the response Deputy Stark heard.

With his handshaking he kept his flashlight on the blonde girl. Her legs were spread open and there looked to be a beer bottle stuck halfway inside her.

Staying back ten feet or so, so he wouldn't mess up the crime scene, he continued to go over the area with his flashlight. Next to the beer bottle on her inner thighs was dark purple and red, looked to him like they might be bite marks, a couple had dried blood around them. The only other marks seem to be around her neck, which was dark blue. Her eyes were open, looking up into the stars and heaven above. He could tell they were also blue, but it was the blue of a bright clear sky, or an amazing lagoon you only see in the movies or a magazine.

The first thing Deputy Stark noticed about the black haired girl, besides her whole face looking like it had been smashed in, was a wound on the left side of her chest, from where he stood it looked like a gunshot wound, then he realized it was a hole were her nipple used to be. Some sick fuck had cut off her nipple, Or bit it off!

"What the fuck!"

He called for his partner again.

"Bob!" Stark yelled.

He couldn't stop looking at this poor girl. She looked to have blood on her left forearm and on her right hand.

Shining his light around the girls, he could see lots of beer bottles, smoked cigarettes, and tons of foot prints. It looked as if there was some kind of party going on here at one time. The girls clothes lay all over and he could see what looked like a purse.

"Rookie, Rookie."

"Over here Bob!" Stark yelled back.

   Bob King was a five-year Deputy Sheriff, and he loved to call his new partner Rookie, and give him as much shit as he could.

"You pissing behind that dumpster? You know they got a bathroom inside" Said Bob.

"Bob just get over here!"

"I don't want to see your little dick Rookie, I got my own, and I don't even like looking at it... what the... What the fuck did you do Rookie?"

"How could you fucking even say that? Look at these poor girls!"

"You're right, you're right sorry Rookie, call for backup" said Bob.

"I did."

"Are they dead?" Asked Bob

"They sure look dead" answered Stark.

"You didn't check?"

"Well I...."

Right at that moment Deputy King saw the short black haired girl's right arm move. Almost at this very same time he heard lots of sirens getting closer.

"She's alive!" Yelled Bob. "Holy shit she's alive. Check the other girl, and watch where you step!"

At 35 years old Homicide Detective for the last five, She thought homicide would be better than gang detail. Justin Scott was already tired of seeing dead bodies, now she would almost pay to go chase around gang bangers.

On her way to the crime scene she went over what info she had so far. What was reported as a double homicide, was now only one. The victims looked to be two teenage girls. One was being transported to Grossmont hospital. She made a mental note to go there next.

William Pike

Justine was not looking forward to any of this! She got to the gas station at 2:15 AM Saturday morning, all seemed quiet except for all the Sheriff cars in the back, and a young Deputy taping off the crime scene with yellow police tape.

Stark was happy to be away from the bodies, and doing something to keep his mind off them. He couldn't believe how stupid he was for not checking their pulses.

He was taping off the crime scene when a white Ford focus pulled up. An attractive woman got out, she was about five foot two, hundred and ten pounds he guessed, she had short dark hair. She was sure a looker. She looked to be headed to the dumpster.

"Ma'am, Ma'am, sorry you can't go over there right now" Stark said.

"And why might that be Deputy?"

She turned toward Deputy Stark and he could now see the detective badge hanging around her neck "Stupid" he could also see the most amazing hazel eyes. How could this five foot two inch girl with the most beautiful hazel eyes be a Homicide Detective?

"Sorry detective, I didn't see your badge."

"That's okay, I'm Detective Scott."

"Deputy Stark.... I was the first on the scene.... I found the girls."

"Well thanks to you one of them is still alive, nice work Stark" said Detective Scott "I'll need to talk to you when I'm done here, stick around. If you can write your report while you're waiting that would be a big help. I'll be headed to the hospital from here"

"Will do Ma'am."

"Just Detective Scott please."

"Okay" said Stark feeling stupid.

Stepping around the cement wall she could see an empty dirt lot, with lots of trees, bushes, and what looked to be bike jumps made out of dirt. The lights the sheriffs set up were very bright, almost as bright as the sun itself. She could see the blonde girl, and within five seconds she pretty much knew what had happened here, every girl's worst nightmare. Somebody had raped and killed this girl, and only God knew what else.

Detective Scott felt sick to her stomach and went down to one knee.

"Detective Scott, you okay?"

Looking up she saw Deputy King "I'm fine King, just looking at something. What do you have for me?"

"Well, the Rookie... I mean Deputy Stark noticed the girls, this one here and the one on the way to the hospital was right next to her on the left. Everything is pretty much the way we found it."

"All these footprints were here?" Asked Scott.

She could tell by looking at them that they were made by boots.

"Yes, that's the way we found it, Stark the EMTs and myself are the only ones to approach the bodies" said King.

Scott noticed a red and white bandana laying on the ground to the left of the blonde girl.

"Did you say that other girl was laying on the left side of this one?" Asked Scott.

"Yes, right on top of that bandana" answered King.

The bandana was folded neatly longways then in half, the way gang members do it, then wear them hanging out of their back pockets to let other gang members know who they are or where they're from. It was stained with something, maybe blood she thought. She put on gloves and then placed the bandana in a plastic bag.

There were lots of beer bottles around and cigarette butts, the girls clothes, a purse, and of course the blonde girl. She looked to be 16 or 17, she was very pretty. Detective Scott was sure she was raped, at least with the beer bottle that was still inside her. She could tell that she had been strangled to death, but she would let the medical examiner decide how the girl died.

As more Sheriffs showed up so did her partner. Homicide Detective Jimmy Johnson, a.k.a. JJ. At six foot four two hundred and sixty pounds, he was the biggest black man

Justine Scott had ever been around, and in this line of work she loved him being her partner. With a bald head and the look of a NFL football player, he took over the room whenever he entered.

"Hey JJ" said Detective Scott.

"What do we got little lady?"

"One hell of a mess big guy."

   She told him what they had so far and then they went to work collecting all the evidence they could, took pictures, made casts of footprints, and sent the body to the morgue. They found a half book of matches with the company name "The Spot Bar and Club" printed on it. Also in the parking lot next to the dumpster they found some tire tracks where someone had peeled out a couple of times, one was wide and the other was not so wide, they were about four feet apart. They took pictures of these too.

   It was 5:30 AM when Detective Scott started to go through the purse. JJ was collecting the report Deputy Stark had wrote, and they were about to head to the hospital. It was the short black haired girl's purse, she could tell this by the school ID she found.

"Peyton Margolin, Santana High School" Scott read out loud.

Margolin? She knew that name and her heart skipped a beat and then picked up the pace. She found a cell phone, makeup, and a wallet, inside the wallet was an emergency contact card and some pictures. She looked at the picture and then the emergency card repeatedly.

"Mother Kim Margolin, Father Tommy Margolin" Scott said.

She couldn't take her eyes off the picture of Tommy with his little girl Peyton. Detective Scott had never seen a smile on Tommy's face before.

Yeah Detective Justine Scott knew the girl's father all right "Tommy Margolin, a.k.a. Tommy guns."

"What do we got there?" asked JJ.

She looked up, with sweaty palms.

"You're not going to believe who this girl's father is."

"Which girl?"

"The one at the hospital" said Scott "Peyton Margolin, Daughter of Tommy guns Margolin."

Chapter 1

The two men walked in the dark along the fence line, looking for the hole they had cut out many years before. Both of them were six foot three inches tall, and were covered from head to toe in camouflage clothing, and even had camouflage face paint on, they looked ready for war. But it was not guns and ammo strapped to their backs and in their hands, it was float tubes and fishing poles.

Yep, they were going fishing. Best friends since they were 15 years old. This was their fishing hole, only it wasn't " their's" in fact you're not even allowed to fish or hunt on this land, it's protected by the federal government, but they didn't care at age fifteen and they don't care at 36 and 37. They got all their camo gear on and won't be seen. If they could just find that damn hole! At 4:30 AM the sun was still not out yet and they were having a tough time finding it.

"Tommy, looks like were going to have to jump it."

"Think you can make it KO?" asked Tommy.

Brandon Smith a.k.a. KO, a.k.a. knockout was six foot three, 270 pounds, and one of the baddest mother fuckers around since his 20s, but he looked really hurt by Tommy's question.

"I'll tell you what Tommy, I'll throw your ass over and then we'll start making old-age jokes."

Tommy started laughing.

"Who said anything about being old?" said Tommy in defense.

They found a good spot and they both jumped the fence as if they were still teenage boys.

"How'd you manage to get out tonight?" asked KO.

"Peyton is staying over at her best friend Suzy's for the weekend."

"Man I've missed fishing, we've had some great times right here" said KO.

"Yeah remember when we were in prison? We would talk about going fishing, well here we are Brother, we're fishing again" Tommy said "we better get in the water before we get caught, we're not the only ones that fish here anymore, and with the bums and the Mexicans living in the bushes, there will be security coming around."

Putting their swimming fins on, and hooking up their fishing poles with some top water poppers, they sneaked into the water, just like when they were kids, the good old days, before all the fights and the killings, before San Diego's biggest and bloodiest gang war, before prison....

To Tommy this sure felt great, fishing with his best friend. Since getting out of prison five years ago they opened a bar together, they named it "The Beach" it has a indoor sand volleyball court, which all the girls played on in bikinis. They both had daughters living at home with them, although KO was still with his wife Gina. Tommy was a single dad, his ex-wife and stripper Kim just couldn't handle the simple life he lived now, so they split up. But life was good.

Tommy took in the view of everything around them, they couldn't hear a sound, the lake was so calm and quiet, it looked like black glass.

"Yep, this is the life" said Tommy to the fish, KO, and whoever could hear him.

KO watched his best friend of over twenty years float in his tube and cast out his fishing pole, he couldn't help but smile, he was proud of Tommy. He didn't think he had it in him to leave the old life behind, all the women, drugs, guns, etc... Sure they talked about it in prison, but he never really believed he could do it. He didn't even go by his nickname Tommy Guns anymore, which he got for having 24 inch arms, along with a couple colt 45s he used to carry around. Boy did they tear this town apart, not that they asked for it, but one thing Tommy Guns didn't put up with was bullies and disrespect, and the Devils did both. God, KO was glad that life was behind them, and most of all he was glad his best friend was still right beside him.

"Got one!" Tom yelled.

"Fuck you" said KO.

Tommy had his fish out of the water and he was laughing like a little kid.

"You owe me five bucks for the first fish" said Tommy.

"What?... we didn't bet" pleaded KO.

"We always bet."

"That was years ago."

"All bets are still the same" said Tommy.

"So you saying if I catch the first bass over 18 inches you're going to stick your dick in it's mouth while I take a picture?" asked KO.

"Yep, just like you did, I still got the picture you know" said Tommy "speaking of 18 inches let's measure this baby."

"No, no, no you can't win two bets with one fish, you know the rules" KO said.

"Whatever" Tommy said as he threw the bass back into the water.

The sun was coming up over the mountains and it shined across the lake, it was going to be a beautiful day.

KO caught the next few bass, but they weren't even close to 18 inches, but it was sure making Tommy nervous. All he could think about was that he had been sitting in cold water now for hours and a picture of his penis next to a 18 inch bass was the last thing he wanted to see.

"What was that?" Tommy said to himself.

There it was again, someone yelling just around the bend.

"Hey KO, you hear that?"

"I thought I heard something" answered KO.

"Sounds like someone is having some trouble" said Tommy.

They paddled their float tubes with the swimming fins on their feet, staying close to the shoreline hidden behind the tall tullys and the bushes. They spotted two teenage boys, who looked to be about the same age as Tommy and KO's Daughters, and three Mexicans in dirty clothes. It looked to Tommy like they were trying to steal the boys fishing poles and tackle box. The next thing he heard confirmed it.

"Let go of my fucking pole!"

The taller of the two boys was holding onto one end of his pole while one of the Mexicans was pulling on the other end.

Tommy and KO creep their way as close as they could without being seen, which was damn close. Tommy found a hole in the tullys and came flying out of his float tube and the lake. It looked to KO like Tommy was shot out of the water by a cannon, water went flying everywhere.

"Buenos Dias Putos!" yelled Tommy.

He kicked the first terrified Mexican in the chest, the swimming fin made a loud slapping sound and the end of it caught the Mexican right under the chin, he went flying backward about five feet. Then Tommy bitch smacked the second closest Mexican, all three took off running as fast as they could.

Tommy was going to ask the boys if they were okay, but all he could hear was KO laughing. KO had a loud infectious laugh, that made everyone around him laugh too, and it was echoing across the lake and through the valley. Tommy and the boys watched KO laugh while he floated in his tube.

"What's so funny?" Asked Tommy.

"Did you see the look on their fucking faces?... You came flying out of the lake, water going everywhere, fins on your feet, camo paint on your face, yelling what kind of sounded like Spanish. They looked like they saw a fucking swamp monster or something about to attack them. I've never seen anyone run so fucking fast!"

It did sound pretty funny and now Tommy and the two boys were laughing as well. For about a minute they all laughed.

"Thank you sir" said the taller of the two boys.

"No problem at all kid. What was that all about?" asked Tommy.

"Not too sure Sir."

"What's with this Sir bizz?"

"Just showing respect Sir... I mean Tommy."

"Tommy... how do you know my name kid?"

Tommy was puzzled... how did this kid know him? Tommy was six foot three, two hundred and twenty pounds, green eyes, shaved head, he had wide shoulders and a slim waist, tattoos covered most of his arms and chest, he did have a small patch of hair under his lower lip, he called it a flavor saver and the ladies loved it "Yeah" Tommy thought to himself "I'm one-of-a-kind."

"Well" said the tall kid "we go to school with your Daughter Peyton, and there's a picture of you, KO, and my Dad on the wall at my house.

"Hmm" said Tommy thinking... "is that right?"

"Yes Sir... I mean Tommy Guns."

Tommy smiled.

"So does Peyton have a Boyfriend at school?"

"Ahhh.... n.. no I don't think so."

"Who's your dad?" Asked Tommy.

"Ken Smith, he said you were all pretty good friends back in the day, he can tell stories about you guys all night long.

I'm Kenny Smith or Junior, this is my best friend Tank or Buddy Thomas"

Tommy looked at the shorter stocky kid, Tank was a good name for him he thought.

"My dad knows you guys too, his name is Sean Thomas" said Tank "He says you used to get more ass than a toilet seat."

Tommy was stunned by this and let it show on his face.

"Use too... I still get more ass than a toilet seat!"

"He said KO could take on Mike Tyson even on his best day."

KO liked this Tank kid already.

"So how's your dad been Kenny?" asked KO as he was getting out of the water.

"He just got out of prison again, this time for gun sales."

"Well send him our love and respect and tell him were still friends, we just... well just tell him hi, and to come by The Beach sometime, that goes for you to Tank" said KO.

"Well I think maybe you Boys should call it a day" said Tommy "those guys might grow some balls and come back."

"Plus standing on the shore is no way to fish this lake" put in KO.

"Okay thanks again" said Kenny.

After the boys left Tommy gave KO a look of distaste.

"What?" asked KO.

"Thanks for the help!"

"What.... you had it under control, plus I can't even jump the fence remember?"

"Whatever" said Tommy "the 18 inch bet is off now!"

"What? Getting scared are you?" taunted KO.

"Whatever!" said Tommy.

William Pike

Chapter 2

Payton could hear voices, they sounded close, so close they could be right next to her. She couldn't open her eyes to check, she couldn't talk, or even move one muscle, or just one little finger. She tried to move her toes.... nope, nothing. "Was she dead?" She must be dead she thought. She couldn't feel any of the pain that she had felt before. "Suzy?" Oh poor Suzy, her best friend in the world... she knew Suzy was dead.. they both must be dead.

"Suzy I'm sorry, I should've never talked to those strangers" but she did talk to them, and then they did the worst things to Suzy and to her, and now.... and now they were both dead. Did you still think when you were dead, or hear people talking, you must she thought, because she could think of nothing else but what those men did to Suzy and to her, it all hurt so bad...

All Suzy and Peyton wanted was to sneak over to the gas station and buy some smokes. That's when she saw the men and the bikes. One of the bikes looked just like her Dad's chopper.

"Hey girls" said one of the men "you wouldn't happen to know the way to Broadway from here would you? We're visiting from Nevada, and were kind of lost"

There were five of them, but Peyton thought the one talking was the best looking of the five. They all looked young though, maybe twenty one to twenty five, but this one had nice eyes and a welcoming smile.

"No we...." Suzy started to say.

"Yes we do" said Peyton "it's about two more miles south down Winter Gardens. You won't be able to miss it."

The young good looking one didn't say anything at first, he just stared at her, from her eyes then all the way down her body.

"All right then, thank you" he finally said.

Peyton and Suzy started to walk away, then Peyton stopped and asked the good-looking one a question.

"Hey you think maybe you could buy some smokes for us?"

"I can do better than that, how about I just give you a pack for the help."

"That would be great" said Peyton smiling.

The young good looking one walked back over to where his friends were just behind the cement wall, and the girls followed. Peyton turned the corner not believing her good luck. Then something hit her hard in the side of the head, so hard it was the last thing she could remember, that is until she woke up...

She could barely open just one of her eyes, but it was enough to see that she was naked, and that there was a man on top of her, hurting her. He had blood on his lips, she didn't know what to do. She never had sex before. Suzy said it would feel good, but all Peyton could feel was pain, then the worst pain of all, the man put her left breast in his mouth and bit off her nipple. The pain was so intense it knocked her out for a second time.

When Payton woke up the second time there was no one on top of her. She still felt a great deal of pain, but she seemed to be numb from the waist down to her toes. She could still just barely open one eye, but she could see Suzy to the right of her, her eyes were wide open and she was not making a sound, not fighting back, just laying there. Her neck was all blue, all the way up to her ears. She was naked with her legs spread open with one of the men's heads between her legs, all she could see of him was his lower back, it said Nevada in big red letters with a white background.

"Times up.... next."

She knew that voice, it was the one she used to think was good looking. The man got up from between Suzy's legs, but then he was replaced by a second man, his head disappeared between Suzy's legs, and all Peyton could see was that word Nevada again.

"Three minutes Dave."

Dave... One of them was named Dave.. some of the things her Dad always told her were starting to come back to her "if anyone ever tries to hurt you, get a name, a license plate number, anything you can think of, write it down" well she had a name, but no way to write it down. A red rag caught her eye, it was laying right next to her. She slowly grabbed it with her right hand and put it under her body. She needed something to write with...

"Times up Dave... Let's get the fuck out of here."

Peyton closed her one eye, she heard beer bottles hitting each other in a toast "Blood and honor!" they yelled.

She heard the bottles being tossed to the ground, the next thing she heard was motorcycle starting up and then taking off.

She tried to call out to Suzy, but her mouth wouldn't open, it hurt so bad she almost passed out again. She needed something to write with... Anything... Peyton touched her right index finger to all the blood on her left breast, right where her nipple used to be, then with the same finger she started to write on her left forearm, she wrote the word Nevada as best she could with one eye and blood on her finger. Dave was the next word she was going to write, but a sharp pain shot through her head and she passed out for the third time.

William Pike

Peyton came to again, she was not too sure how much time had passed, this time she couldn't open her eyes at all, but she could hear people talking.

"The blonde girl is dead."

No... no.. not Suzy.... she can't be dead, we were just going to get some smokes.

Chapter 3

"Tommy Guns Margolin" said Detective Justine Scott.

Detective Scott had a real bad feeling about this.

"I never heard of him" said JJ.

"Well, he's been out of the loop for about ten years now, he went to prison and did five years out of ten for manslaughter. He got out about five years ago, and has pretty much stayed low-key every since, stays home or he's at his bar."

"That don't tell me much" replied JJ.

"Okay, let me take you back to the beginning, as you know before I joined homicide I was with the gang unit, so I got all the dirt."

"Tommy Margolin had two best friends, Brandon Smith, a.k.a. knockout, a.k.a. KO, and Benny Tula. They had all been friends since high school. They were tough kids who earn their respect on the streets as they got older and bigger, although Benny Tula stopped growing at about five foot eight, one hundred and eighty pounds, but his mouth more than made up for his size. They pretty much stayed out of trouble in high school, they all played football and work for Brandon's Dad after school and in the summertime at his custom motorcycle shop.

The trouble didn't start till they were twenty one and started hitting the bar scene. They all had their own custom choppers by this time, and before you knew it they started their own motorcycle club, just the three of them, they called themselves Iron Cowboys. The local law didn't really consider them a gang, not at first anyways.

They were known as bad asses, and they didn't take shit from no one, they were never bullies and never started the trouble, they were the total opposite in fact, and because of this they were popular with everyone. All the girls would sing that song "save a horse, ride a cowboy" by John Rich. They lived by three words, that you would hear them yell from time to time during a toast or whatnot "Drink, Fight, Fuck!" And that's what they did until the summer of 1999, when Benny Tula was murdered."

"It all started on a Saturday night a local biker bar called Full Throttle, where one of the biggest motorcycle gangs hung out, the Devils. There happened to be two of them there that night, young loudmouth punks, who preyed on the weak and the loners. If I remember right it was about

1:00 AM an hour before closing time. The girls were all dancing, the boys were downing shot after shot, when the Devils found their prey for the night, a youngster about Benny's size playing pool with his girl. Tommy Guns was sick of seeing this shit, and tonight he wasn't going to let it fly. He came up behind the group next to the pool table. The two Devils were wearing black boots, jeans with black leather chaps, black shirts, and their black leather vests with their patches on them that said Devils across the top, California across the bottom, and had a picture of a demon in the middle with 666 on its forehead, the letters and picture were all in green over black, which were their gang colors green and black.

"I see you two have met my brother-in-law" Tommy said as he winked to the prey and his girl.

"This don't have anything to do with you Iron Cowboys, so fuck off!" said one of the Devils.

"Well I say it does!" came the voice of KO.

Who of course always followed his brothers lead.

Tommy could see Benny talking to some girls, not even knowing what was going on. Tommy could tell it was Benny because he had his patch on, Iron Cowboys across the top, San Diego on the bottom, and a picture of three Cowboys holding six shooters in the middle. Benny was a lover not a fighter anyhow and Tommy almost smiled thinking about it.

"Well, what seems to be the problem?" Tommy asked.

With the odds being more even, the Devils tone changed a little bit.

"Well he said we look gay" said one of the Devils.

Tommy just couldn't picture this kid saying that.

"Well are you gay? I never see you two talking to any of the girls in this shit hole!"

"You best watch your fucking mouth Cowboy!"

"Or what?" said KO coming closer.

"Oh you'll see" the Devil said.

The Devils backed down and made their way to the exit.

"Thanks for the help guys" said the prey.

"Did you call them gay?" asked Tommy

"No, I was telling my girl that if I wore that much leather I would look like I was gay, not that I have anything against gays."

Tommy smiled at this, if the kid didn't have a girl with him, Tommy would almost bet money that he was gay.

"Let me buy you guys a drink for the help."

"Sure thing" said KO.

About a half hour later the bar was starting to close down. Benny was outside in the parking lot, he was already on his bike and ready to go, Tommy and KO were waiting for two girls who wanted to "ride a cowboy instead of a horse" As the girls came out they fired up their choppers.

"Race you to the house!" yelled Benny.

He took off like a bat out of hell, they could hear his pipes screaming down the street, getting farther and farther away, when the gunshots rang out in the night, lots of gunshots five, seven, Tommy lost count. Leaving the girls behind Tommy and KO took off after Benny. About two miles down the road they saw Benny's chopper in the middle of the street, Benny lay on the side of the street with his head up against the sidewalks curb, his neck was turned at an impossible angle, his body was full of bullet holes"

"That was the night the war started between the Iron Cowboys and the Devils. In the next six months many would die" said Detective Scott.

After they lay Benny to rest, Tommy could think of nothing else but revenge. They were outnumbered hundreds to two, even though there was only nine Devils in the San Diego chapter, he wanted them all dead. But first they would deal with the San Diego chapter, so they started to make plans. The first plan was to shoot up the Devils clubhouse, while they were in it of course. The clubhouse was on a main Street and would be impossible to open fire on without being seen. No matter how bad they wanted revenge, they didn't want to get life in prison. Tommy thought it would be nice to have a remote control assault rifle, and that's exactly what he built.

Using a fully automatic AK-47 rigged with the insides of a remote control car. He made the arm that use to turn the front wheels a arm that pulled the trigger back into firing position, once got that working he attached to metal poles about ten inches long to the barrel and the stock of the rifle. Then using a shallow plastic storage container, he filled it with quick dry cement and settled the two poles holding the AK-47 into the cemented. The finished product was a freestanding fully automatic remote control assault rifle.

Once they finished, they waited till 3:00 AM on Friday morning and placed it on top of a business right across the street from the Devils clubhouse, they aimed it right where they wanted it and left.

Tommy Guns and KO return that night at about 10:30 PM, only they weren't across the street, they were a block away sitting in a car with the remote in Tommy's hands.

By 11:00 PM the clubhouse was alive with Devils. They could count seven bikes and four Devils out front smoking, but they knew there were more inside.

"What do you think KO?"

"Fuck'em!"

Tommy guns turned the wheel on the remote which pulled the trigger back. Sixty rounds came flying out within seconds, bodies were laying in a pile right in front of the door to the clubhouse, right where they aimed the AK-47. The Devils that were trying to run out got hit and the ones outside trying to run in got hit. It was better than they could have ever dreamed. They started the car and drove away.

Five Devils died that night, and one was rushed to the hospital with multiple bullet wounds.

Everyone knew it was the Iron Cowboys that did it, but no one knew for sure, not the Cops or the Devils, but the Devils would soon figure out it was the Iron Cowboys.

Four months later two more Devils would die. The details are not all known, but a pipe bomb went off at a rest stop off the I-8 freeway, westbound, at midnight on a Wednesday. It was said that the Devils wanted to set up a meeting with the Iron Cowboys to sort out their problems. Tommy and KO smelled an ambush, so they just drove through the rest stop and tossed out a two pound pipe bomb covered in ball bearings.

A trucker would find the bodies at 12:45 AM his statement in the police report read "the two bodies looked like Swiss cheese, and there was no more restroom where it should have been, but there were shitters everywhere."

The Cops still couldn't put a finger on Tommy Guns and KO.

There were only two Devils left in the San Diego chapter. The President Ronnie Gutterman, a.k.a. Axe, and Steve Sands, a.k.a. Sandman. They both refused any police protection. The Sandman was still laid up at home from his ten gunshot wounds he got at the clubhouse, and Axe was not seen very much out in public. In fact Devils support shirts, green and black rags, or anything else were not seen in any bars or on the streets. Tommy Guns and KO had the town on lockdown.

Axe would try to get some out-of-state help from other Devils chapters, but it wouldn't come in time.

   Almost six months after Benny Tula was gunned down Tommy and KO were driving westbound down Highway 52, on their way to a party at about 9 p.m. on a Saturday night. They were cruising along in Tommy's Ford F350 crew cab truck when their prayers were answered. Axe, President of the Devils came riding by in the fast lane with his patch on. Without the patch they would've never even knew who he was. It had to be faith Tommy thought.

"Look what we have here KO"

"Holy shit!"

KO jumped into the back seat and pulled out a pistol grip pump action 12 gauge shotgun from under the seat, and rolled his window down. Tommy caught up to the bike, rolled his window down and yelled out the window.

"Hey stupid.... hey stupid!"

Axe Looked over at him.

"You know you got a fucking target on your back?"

Tommy could see his eyes open wide as Axe saw KO in the back window.

"Boom!"

The 12 gauge exploded lifting Axe right off his bike and smashing him into the K-rail. Tommy could hear his bones cracking and breaking on impact. This would put both Tommy Guns and KO in prison.

The police had a witness this time, and although they didn't know the make and model of the truck, they remembered reading the sticker in the back window. "We may be Cowboys, but we're Charger fans!" They arrested Tommy and KO the next day, but with not that much hard evidence and the witnesses now knowing who the shooters were, didn't want to come to court. Tommy and KO got a deal for manslaughter, ten years with no strikes. Not a bad deal huh?"

"Not at all" said JJ "so Peyton was seven years old when Tommy Margolin went to prison?"

"Yeah and KO's little girl was six" said Detective Scott "it was the year 2000 when they got prison. There may have only been nine Devils on the streets of San Diego, but there would be more in prison..."

Chapter 4

When Tommy Guns Margolin and Brandon K.O Smith arrived at Richard J. Donovan prison in San Diego County, they were somewhat celebrities. Their case along with the seven other murdered Devils had been closely watched on the news channels for the last two months. Everybody knew who the Iron Cowboys were, from the correctional officers to the inmates.

Tommy Guns and KO took prison in stride, without missing a step. Donovan has four prison yards, 1, 2, 3, and 4 yard. The 4 yard was their first stop, as it is with every inmate that comes to Donovan. It's called the reception yard. They were placed in building 16, also known as 16 block. There they would stay in their cells 24 hours a day, while that institution evaluated their physical and mental health, and worked out their classification scores, which was based on the crime you committed, and other things. A score of 1–19 was level I, 20–30 level II, 31–40 level III and over 40 level four. After you completed that you were moved to one of the other four buildings on the 4 yard, where you would stay and wait, sometimes for months to get shipped to one of the other thirty two prisons in California.

Tommy Guns Margolin, now Inmate number K15840, and Brandon knockout Smith, now Inmate number K15848 were classified as level III with 35 points each. They were sent to 18 block, where they would wait to see what prison they would go to or if they would just stay at Donovan.

While in 18 block they got to go to yard once a day for an hour with the other thousand inmates from building 17, 18, 19, 20 and the gym. The yard has a half mile long track to walk or run around, with grass in the middle for sports, it also had a basketball court, handball court, pull-up bars, and dip bars that the inmates could all use.

   On their first day of yard it didn't take them long to meet all of the other white inmates on the yard that day. In prison Whites stick with Whites, Blacks with Blacks, Mexicans with Mexicans, and Others with Others. But it was wise to show respect to everyone or you could end up with a piece of steel in your neck.

One Inmate Tommy and KO met on that first day was Tiny. Tiny was anything but tiny, he was a fellow outlaw biker who ran with the club Warlords, out of the Los Angeles chapter, who were also enemies with the Devils, and every other well-known biker gang. But Tiny didn't seem to want trouble with the Iron Cowboys, in fact it was just the opposite, he wanted to be friends. Tommy remembered as saying his favorite writer David Gemel would often write "The enemy of my enemies, must therefore be my friends"

That quick made friendship might have saved Tommy and KO's life's, because after they all shook hands and had a little small talk, Tiny had some important news for them.

"Animals got a piece of steel, and he's been putting the word out that your dead men when you got here"

"Who is Animal?" asked Tommy.

"Devils, LA chapter" answered Tiny.

"What's he look like?"

"Oh you can't miss him, long red hair, with a red beard, and he's about my size" said Tiny.

"What are you seven foot?" asked KO.

"Six foot ten, three hundred pounds."

Not more than thirty seconds later they spotted Animal walking their way around the track. He had two other Inmates following behind him, but as they got closer the other two fell back. Tommy, KO, and Tiny knew Animal was making his move. Without a word KO started walking right towards Animal.

As KO got closer to Animal they locked eyes and KO knew there would be no talking to this Animal. By God he was big. At about ten feet apart Animal pulled a makeshift knife out from behind his back, it was about eight inches long. KO's heart was pounding, but he picked up his pace, which seem to throw Animal off. The knife was in his left hand. At the last moment KO sidestep to Animals right and hit him with a right uppercut. He put all his two hundred and seventy pounds into it. The impact was so hard and loud it snapped Animals head back and he was lifted off his feet making him land on the back of his head.

Some would say that Animal was dead before he even hit the ground, later they would hear that Animal died of a broken neck. KO never stopped to look, he just kept walking as if nothing had happened, leaving Tommy and Tiny standing there awestruck.

There were no more Devils on the 4 yard, and they had no other problems, though they heard a rumor that there was a Devil on the 1 yard, which Tiny would soon be moved too. Two months later Tommy and KO would also be placed on the 1 yard, but the first thing on their minds was not the Devil, who went by the name Chopper. Nope they were thinking about getting married to their Daughters Moms, Kim and Gina. Tommy for sure didn't like being without a woman for so long.

It was Tiny again a month later who would bring them the news that Chopper was losing face and respect for not taking revenge for all his dead Brother's that have died at the hands of the Iron Cowboys.

"I think he is going to make a move" Tiny said "I was told he got a piece of steal from a guy who works in the welding shop."

"Man this is bad timing, KO and I are supposed to get married in two weeks" said Tommy.

"Yeah this is not good" put in KO.

Tiny could see that they were taking this news hard. He also knew how badly they wanted to see their Daughters and Old ladies at a family visit.

"Well, tell you what, I'll go have a talk with Chopper, see if we can settle this some other way" said Tiny.

"Thanks Tiny, but don't get yourself in a wreck over this" said Tommy.

"I'll let you guys know what he says."

That night Choppers cellmate came home from working in the kitchen to find Chopper hanging in his cell by a rope made out of a sheets. When Tommy and KO went to Tiny's cell in the morning he denied it all, but Tommy and KO could see that Tiny only had one sheet left on his bed.

Everyone in the prison would still think Tommy and KO killed Chopper too. That would make ten dead Devils, and from that day on Tommy and KO would run and call shots for all the whites in that prison. Every Devil who showed up at Donovan would place themselves into protective custody.

Things went smooth for the next three and a half years. Although the prison wouldn't allow Tommy and KO to be cellmates, they were only two cells apart. With less than a year and a half left before they paroled, two odd things would happen, well odd to Tommy and KO. The first would be a visit from HBO. They were doing a special on murderers. "Men who murdered" and they wanted to asked Tommy and KO some questions, which they would pay them both $20,000 dollars each for. Tommy and KO had big plans to open their own bar when they got out, so they said yes to HBO.

They would say many things on that HBO show "Men who murder" but the one question-and-answer HBO would use for their pilot of this show, and would be seen all around the world with this one.

"It's said that you guys have killed ten men, the public wants to know why, and how does it make you feel inside to know the hurt you caused their families and loved ones?"

Tommy responded first.

"Wow, that's a pretty deep question. First off we've only been convicted of killing one man, the others are still open cases and we cannot comment on them. How do I feel inside, well I guess I feel bad about maybe not going to heaven, and I think about going to hell for what I've done, then one day a friend of ours named Tiny was talking with me about it. He tried to set my mind at ease, he told me "men bring war to other men, other countries, the United States has Navy, Army etc. they go to war to protect their families and the people of the United States by shooting, bombing, and killing, we all call them heroes, and when they die, we say that they went to a better place… Heaven."

I thought about what Tiny had told me. The Devils brought this war to the Iron Cowboys and they paid the price. Do I feel bad? Yeah I feel bad for our best friend Benny Tula, age twenty six, who was shot down in the middle of the street, that's what I feel bad about!" Said Tommy.

"And what about you Mr. Smith?"

"Kill my family, I'll kill yours, Heaven, Hell? As long as my Brother is by my side, I don't really care much where I go!" Said KO.

The next visit would be from a lawyer, a lawyer sent by the Devil's National President. It seemed the local law wasn't the only ones worried about Tommy Guns and KO getting out of prison.

"Mr. Margolin, Mr. Smith, I'm here on behalf of the Devils motorcycle club, to see if we could come to some kind of agreement for a truce between the Iron Cowboys and the Devils"

"Is that so?" Said Tommy.

"Yes sir it is. I have with me a simple contract written by the National President himself, along with a statement."

Tommy read it first "I would first like to say that I never declared war against the Iron Cowboys. Benny Tula was shot down by Cowards, who brought death to their Brothers. If you agree to call a truce, I will agree to expel the Devils San Diego chapter"

After KO read it they both agreed to the truce.

William Pike

With two months left till Tommy and KO paroled, the local law was not aware of any truce and they were still not looking forward to more blood on the San Diego streets.

The local gang unit teamed up with the Institutional Gang Investigation unit, a.k.a. I. G. I, at Donovan prison, to see what Tommy Guns and KO were planning after their release. They placed a jailhouse snitch in between Tommy and KO's cells to get information. In his report it read "all they talked about was opening a bar and calling it The Beach, spending time with their Daughters, and going fishing."

They both paroled in 2005 and have been doing just that, not one problem.

"Well that's one heck of a story" said JJ.

"Yeah it was a little wild around here back then" said Detective Scott.

"How do you think Mr. Margolin is going to take the news?" Asked JJ.

"I don't know, and we still don't know who the blonde girl is yet."

"Okay let's leave the Forensic team to wrap this up. I'll go to Mr. Margolins, while you go to the hospital and see what they got on Peyton, then I'll meet you there" said JJ.

"Sounds like a good plan."

"Okay see you there then" said JJ.

Chapter 5

Detective Justine Scott was heavy hearted as she drove south down Winter Gardens to the I–8 freeway. "Who could do that to those poor girls?" Even without the reports from the M.E and forensics, she could tell it was a gang rape. She was guessing maybe five to six men. And the red and white bandana, was it a gang who gang raped them? There were only two gangs that wore red and white in San Diego. So if that was the case it would narrow it down for her. She passed Broadway and Winter Gardens turned into Second Street. People were just starting their days at 6:00 AM on this Saturday morning. The sun was up and the skies were clear, it could've been a beautiful San Diego day if it hadn't started out the way it had. She made a right onto the I–8 and headed west toward Grossmont hospital. "Had the girls been out drinking with a group of boys, and then things went wrong?" With all the beer bottles and smoked cigarettes all around, it sure looked like they were hanging out.

The gas station worker didn't start work till 12:00 AM, and he said he didn't notice anything, but at that time at night he never went outside or behind the building, and there were no cameras back there. She made a note to talk with the second shift worker A.S.A.P. Traffic was light and she made it to the hospital within ten minutes. She hoped Peyton was still alive and able to talk.

She pushed the button and got a parking ticket. Parking was easy to find this early, so she parked on the first floor of the underground parking garage. She went to the front desk where she showed her I.D and was told that Peyton was moved to the ICU, room 312, but they had her name down as Jane Doe. Scott told the Nurse her real name, Peyton Margolin, and then headed to the room 312 in ICU.

In ICU she walked to the Nurse's station, asked for the treating Doctor for room 312, and also gave the Nurse Peyton's proper name. She walked to room 312 while the Doctor was being paged.

312 was a private room, with one bed, a chair, T.V, a connecting bathroom, and a window looking out towards the West. Peyton was motionless, she had no more hair, her head had been shaved. Her head was about twice the size as it should have been, she had a tube coming out of her skull, it was draining blood and fluid, both eyes were swollen shut, and her nose also had tubes in it, her lips were split, and she had dried blood at the corners of her mouth.

Detective Justine Scott felt a lump in her throat and tears building up in her eyes, when the Doctor walked in.

"Hello there, I'm Dr. Fouts."

"Homicide Detective Justine Scott."

"Homicide?"

"Yes, well… there's another girl… she didn't make it" said Scott.

"Oh, I see, well this young lady is very lucky" Said Dr. Fouts "I have a full report here for you, would you like me to go over it with you?"

"Yes, that would be good."

"Well, let's start with her injuries. She has massive head trauma, as you can see, which is putting pressure on her brain. We drilled a hole in her skull and inserted a intraventricular catheter to relieve the pressure. She has a broken nose, eye socket, and jaw, that all needed surgery, which I did myself. She has been intubated and placed on a ventilator in a induced coma for her body to rest and heal for now. Her areola on her left breast, or her nipple, was bitten off. There was not much I could do for that. Before this rape it is my opinion that this young lady was a virgin, there is some tearing of tissue. We found two types of semen, and two types of DNA from saliva. We also took pictures, we believe the weapons used to cause the head injuries were steel toe boots, as you'll see in the pictures, they stomped and kicked this poor girl and they left bloody boot prints on her face and head."

The doctor paused for a minute to let that all settle in, and then he continued.

"We also took pictures of her right hand and left forearm, although there were no injuries there, there was blood, mostly on her right index finger, and on her left forearm, the word Nevada was spelled out in blood… the word was wrote in her own blood. I'm not a Detective, but I would guess she wrote it herself."

Scott began to sort through all this new information and didn't know what to say. "Nevada?" was that someone's name?"

"Thank you Dr. Fouts, you've done an amazing job."

"Anything else I can do for you Detective?"

"There is one thing, I would like to keep the details classified for now, to the press and even her family."

"She's a minor, and we must tell her parents" said Dr. Fouts.

"I understand Doctor, but this is a very sensitive situation, and we don't want her Father to know the details yet."

"Very well Detective, I shall leave the report to just the injuries."

"Thank you Doctor."

Chapter 6

Detective Johnson got into his 2008 Chrysler 300 and looked at the address and phone number that he got off Peyton Margolin's emergency card. "922 Second St. Santee, CA 92071" if his memory served him right that was right by Santana high school. Just to make sure, he punched the address into his GPS system.

JJ loved his Chrysler 300, it was dark blue, had 22 inch wheels, and was powered by a Hemi. He had a department car, but every time it was time to leave the house to go to work, he could not help but walk straight to his 300.

"Yes, right by Santana high school" he said to himself.

He pulled out of the gas station and turned right on Pepper street and headed west towards Santee.

JJ's thoughts were on his partner Justine Scott as he drove. He could tell working homicide was starting to get to her. Although she was a great detective, as many are, but not all are cut out for homicide. He started noticing the change in her, on their last case. To be honest it got to JJ a little too.

They were called to a mobile home park after a report from a neighbor, saying that that place next door smelled as if someone had died. After the police checked, there indeed was someone dead. When JJ and Justine showed up, they could smell it right away. All the police officers were outside and all the way across the street. JJ heard one of them say "that's why they get paid the big bucks" they entered through the front door, to the left was the kitchen, to the right the living room, the two bedrooms were to the back, but they would not make it there till later.

Just in front of the TV laying on the floor in the middle of the living room, which was broadcasting Jerry Springer, was an older woman in her fifties. Her stomach was cut open from her pelvic bone to her chest down, either someone had pulled all her inside out, or the fifteen cats that were feeding on them pulled them out as they ate her.

They found her husband that night drunk at a local bar. He gave a confession with a smile on his face the whole time.

"Every day, every fucking day she would bring home another fucking cat! I'd see missing cat signs up by the mailboxes, on poles all around. She was bringing all the cats she could find, they would piss and shit everywhere. She was spending what little money we had on cat food, fucking cat food! Well, I just thought of a way to feed all those cats and save my money at the same time… Pretty smart huh?"

JJ and Justine were blown away by the confession.

William Pike

"How could someone do that to their own wife JJ?"

"I don't know little lady."

JJ could tell that she had not let that case go yet, and this morning he could see that lost look in her eyes, like she was thinking about the past. She once told him that she was attacked and almost raped in high school...

Justine was having a good time with the girls, it was Saturday night and they were at the skateboard park, watching all the boys act cool. The skate park was at an outside park located inside a big public park. It stayed open until 10:00 PM on Friday and Saturday, which was the time she was supposed to be home by. At 9:30 she said goodbye to the girls and headed home. It was a shorter walk to cut across the park, and that was what she did.

As she passed some big oak trees, and man grabbed her from behind, she could smell the sour wine on his breath as he spoke to her.

"Don't say a frucking word!"

"What are you doing? Let me go!" Justine cried out.

He hit her violently in the face and threw her to the ground.

"No, no,... Stop please" she begged.

"I said shut up bitch" he yelled as he tore off her clothes.

"No please, no, no, don't."

She tried to fight back, but she was trapped under his body weight, he hit her again, hard, so hard all she could see was a flash of bright light, then the stars in the night sky. As the man sat up to undo his belt he was hit in the face with a football.

"What the fuck!" He yelled.

"They teach us in school that no means no asshole!" Said a tall boy with his two friends.

Before the sick rapist could do anything the tall boys friend kicked him in the face.

Before Justine knew it all three boys were kicking the shit out of the man.

The tall boy got on his knees beside her.

"Are you okay?" he asked.

He had the most beautiful green eyes. Justine had seen this boy in school, he was two years older and the quarterback of the football team. She didn't know what to say, he was 2two years older, she just kept looking into his beautiful eyes, and she knew she was in love with this boy and owed him her life.

"Here put this on."

He took off his letterman's jacket and gave it to her. She put it on and it fell to her knees.

"What do you want to do with this guy Tommy?" said one of his friends.

William Pike

Yes, that was his name, Tommy Margolin. She wondered what her name would sound like "Justine Margolin" she liked that.

"I don't know, let's ask her" Tommy said.

"You got a name?"

"Justine Marg... I mean Justine Scott."

"Are you okay Justine? What do you want to do about this?" Asked Tommy "if you want to call the cops, we'll have to take off, we've been drinking and coach won't like that."

"I got a better idea" said Justine.

They stripped the unconscious man out of all this clothes, and using all their belts and the man's, they strapped him to one of the oak trees standing up. Justine took some lipstick out of her purse and wrote across the man's chest and stomach "I like to rape little girls!" After that she drew back her right foot and she kicked the man in the balls over and over till Tommy took a hold of her, she was crying, Tommy stood there and hugged her, he told her it was okay and lightly kissed her on top of her head.

He left the other boys at the Park and walked Justine all the way home, at her door he handed her all of her tore up clothes and told her she could just keep the jacket, she gave him a hug.

"Thank you Tommy."

"Anytime Justine, and don't worry we won't tell a soul about any of this."

Then he turned and walked away.

"Bye Tommy, I love you" she said, but not loud enough for him to hear.

She was fifteen at the time, and she still had Tommy's jacket.

   JJ turned right on Magnolia and is GPS said "continue on Magnolia for six miles" he hoped Justine would pull through, maybe he should have went to the hospital instead of sending her. He turned right on Second street and drove to 922.

It was a well-kept house with a long driveway off the street, the house was a two-story, painted light tan with white trim. There was a man getting out of a new BMW 5 series, and what looked to be another man waiting in another BMW. JJ hated this part of the job. He took a deep breath and got out of his car.

"Nice ride" said the man.

"Thanks, are you Mr. Margolin?" asked JJ.

"No sir, but you got the right house, were just delivering this car."

"Is Mr. Margolin here?"

"No sir, he's gone fishing for the day. He bought this car for his Daughter, told us to drop it off today because she wouldn't be home. It's a surprise present for her graduation, some present don't you think?"

"I would say so, thanks for the info, I'll leave him a card" said JJ.

The man left and JJ walked to the door and knocked just to make sure, there was no answer. He left his card and then tried the phone number. It was not a cell phone, and he could hear the house phone starting to ring. He left a short message to call, and then walked back to the car.

In the car he called Justine at the hospital.

"Homicide, Detective Scott."

"It's JJ."

"Hey how did it go?" Asked Justine.

"Struck out, nobody home but a man dropping off a new BMW 5 series."

"Really, he must be doing pretty good these days"

"Yeah so good it's for his seventeen year old Daughter" said JJ "and from what the delivery guy said, Mr. Margolin is off fishing for the day"

"Did you call?"

"Yeah it was the house number."

"Well, that's all we can do for now" said Justine "I'm still at the hospital, Peyton is in pretty bad shape, but the Doctor says she'll pull through. As of right now she's in a coma."

"How are you holding up?" Asked JJ.

"What's that supposed to mean JJ?"

"Nothing… you just seem tired and not yourself at the crime scene."

"Yeah well I am tired, it's about 7:00 AM and we've been up all night" said Justine.

"You're right, I'm just worried thats all, said JJ "how about we take a break, wait for the reports, and for Mr. Margolin to call. I'll meet you at the department at 12:00 PM unless we get a break."

"Sounds like a plan, sorry for biting your head off JJ."

Justine knew JJ was right, the job was getting to her, and this was the worst, standing in this hospital room with Peyton, who is part of Tommy. She didn't want to leave Peyton by herself. She sat down in the chair, put her head back, and sleep took over her body at once. She dreamed of high school… And she dreamed of Tommy…

Chapter 7

It was a little after 11:00 AM, the sun was high in the sky, beating down on Tommy and KO, Tommy had caught six bass, and KO had caught eight, not one was eighteen inches and they both seemed relieved. The fish had stopped biting, and Tommy's legs were killing him, they had been paddling around the lake for seven hours now, and twice they had to hide from the security that checks on the lake. To KO that was the best part about fishing here. They would paddle as fast as they could when they heard the security truck coming, they would paddle their float tubes deep into the tullys and not move a muscle or say a word. KO would always start giggling and laughing just like a little kid would do. This security never had a chance at catching them, not with all their camouflage gear on.

"What do you say KO, you want to call it a day?"

"Yeah we could do that, you owe me ten dollars for catching the most fish though" KO bragged.

"Yeah, yeah, add it to my bill."

They paddled to the shore and packed all their fishing gear, then started the hike to the truck.

"I sure hope we can find that hole in the fence" Tommy said.

It was going to be a little harder to jump the fence tired and all wet.

"If not I could still throw you over" KO joked. "What are your plans for the rest of the day?" asked KO.

"No plans, I just have to hide Peyton's new BMW in the garage, but she won't be home till tomorrow."

"I can't believe you bought her a new BMW! You know you fucked me right? My Wife and Daughter are going to both want one now!"

Laughing Tommy said "I never thought about that, sorry bro…"

"Whatever" said KO "how about we go back to my place, cleanup, go check on the bar, grab some lunch, and a drink?"

"Yeah that sounds good, did you see the new Hostess I hired?" asked Tommy.

"When are you going to stop fucking all these college girls and find a new wife?"

"As soon as one of them marries me" Tommy said with a smile.

"Hey don't bring up the BMW if the family's home, I don't want to hear it yet."

William Pike

They found the hole in the fence, and after a ten minute. walk they got to the truck, loaded all their gear and headed to KO's.

   KO lived just past Tommy's house by about a mile on El Nopal street, in a three-bedroom house, with a three car garage, with a separate garage for their choppers. They seemed to always be there working on them or changing the parts for newer, cooler parts that always cost more money. Even though they didn't ride them much these days, and they put away their Iron Cowboy patches away for good. That life was in the past, but they still loved to ride every now and then. They made it to KO's and Tommy could see KO smile when he saw that his Wife's car was gone.

"Home Sweet home."

"KO I don't understand why you're even married."

"What you mean? In-house pussy is the best."

"You got problems!"

"Tommy if women threw themselves at me like they do you, I would be a happy single man, but they don't, and there's nothing like coming home at night and finding my Wife in bed waiting for me, and there's nothing like coming home on a Saturday afternoon and finding her not at home either, so let's clean up, jump on the bikes and get the fuck out of here before she shows up and I get stuck fixing something."

Tommy was laughing so hard he couldn't even get any words out of his mouth.

They showered, put on clean clothes, and in less than ten minutes they were in the garage with their choppers. Tommy had a black 1998 custom chopper, it had drag bars, 80 spoked chrome wheels, 250 series back tire, 113 inch S&S motor, with a 5 speed tranny, and with short drag pipes, that you could hear for miles. KO had a 1996 Harley-Davidson custom soft tail, painted gray with white pin stripping, eighteen inch ape hangers, and white wall tires. When he sat on it and reached up to those eighteen inch handlebars he looked like he was flying down the road. They fired the two bikes up, let them warm, and took off as if KO just saw his Wife come home with a to do list.

The Beach was the idea they had for a bar while they were in prison. And after they did the HBO special, they could talk about nothing else for the last six months of their prison term. Tommy and KO wanted to open a place that would draw a young college crowd, not the riffraff or dive bar type drunks. They found a place off that I–8, on College Boulevard a mile away from San Diego State University. It was perfect, big enough to do what they always talked about. They had two bars inside, the main bar, and the back bar, four pool tables, dance floor, and their favorite, the volleyball court, complete with sand and a net around it to stop any balls from wreaking havoc. To play volleyball you had to have a team of four or two, mixed with women and men, or just all women. All players must wear board shorts or bikinis to play. You could play any night of the week for fun or practice, and on Sundays they had a volleyball tournament which always packed the bar. Once a month on whatever night Tommy and KO thought was the best, they would have a beach party. They would set up beer kegs all around the bar, and pass out plastic cups to customers dressed in their beachwear, which they could fill and drink as much beer as they wanted for only $10 dollars. Tommy and KO never thought they would do so well, but The Beach was the most popular bar among the college kids.

Tommy and KO pulled into their parking spots and walked inside, the first thing Tommy noticed was the new Hostess he hired was not at work, then he noticed the four women playing volleyball "very nice" there was a good crowd at 12:00 PM on a Saturday. They walked to the main bar.

"What's up Cindy?" Tommy said.

Cindy was one of the Bartenders, at twenty five years old, with long blonde hair, grayish blue eyes, double D breast, she was the favorite Bartender for any man who came into The Beach.

"Well, look who finally showed up to work."

"We don't really work here Cindy we just kind of own the place" KO said with a smile.

"Plus we went fishing today, you should've been there Cindy in a bikini. If KO would of won the eighteen inch bet, I would of let you take the picture."

"What's that supposed to mean?" asked Cindy.

"Forget it, how was business last night" Tommy asked laughing.

"It was real good, and you guys missed out on some really good volleyball games. There was two college girls that were beating everyone's ass."

"Two girls?"

"Yeah they played topless all night, it was some show."

"Dammit!...I always miss the good shit!" said KO really meaning it.

"Whip me and KO up two red bull vodkas" said Tommy.

"You boys don't get to drunk or I might pull one of you into the office and see if I can get a raise out of you."

"Oh you'll get a raise alright" Tommy said smiling.

He was going to say more when the phone behind the bar rang.

"The Beach, Cindy speaking... one minute please... It's for you Tommy."

"Hello."

"Tommy, it's Suzy Simpsons Dad Frank, have you seen or talked to Peyton or Suzy today?"

Chapter 8

Frank Simpson is a 42-year-old car salesman for El Cajon Ford in East County San Diego, and like most car salesman, Saturday is his busy day. The alarm clock went off, and he turned it off as fast as he could, so that it wouldn't wake up his seven month pregnant wife. The clock read 6:30 AM. Frank rolled over and kissed his wife on the forehead, and then gave the baby belly a light kiss.

He went to the connecting master bathroom shaved, showered, and brushed his teeth. Then he picked out a nice pair of gray slacks, a white long sleeve shirt, and a grey tie with yellow stripes. He walked through his three-bedroom two bath condo towards the kitchen, on the way down the hall he noticed that Suzy's bedroom door was open. He took a quick peek inside, there was her four post bed, two night stands, a dresser, and the computer desk, the computers screensaver had that young man from the Twilight movie on it. The bed was all made up, and

Peyton's bag still sat on top of the pink covers. Thinking maybe they'll fell asleep playing the PlayStation 3 all night he went to the living room. There was no sign of the girls, and the TV showed the PlayStation 3 was on pause. Suzy's purse was on the coffee table. Suzy never got up before at least 10:00 AM on the weekends, Frank thought it was strange that the girls were not in the house at 7:00 in the morning. He went to the kitchen and put some coffee on. The two tickets to the Black Eyed Peas were still on the refrigerator, they are playing at the Cox Arena tonight and the girls were excited about going. Waiting for his coffee he checked the guest room, it was empty. He went to look out front, the front door was unlocked, and Suzy's keys were hanging by the door. There was no sign of the girls outside. Walking back in the kitchen, Frank grabbed the phone and called Suzy's cell phone, he heard it ringing in her purse. The T.V and video game on, purse and phone left on the table, and with her keys left in the house, Frank was starting to get the feeling that the girls were up to no good. He remembered all too well what it was like to be seventeen. Maybe they were at one of those boy's houses in the complex. He left a note for Suzy to call him at work, and told her he would be holding onto the Black Eyed Peas tickets until he heard from her. He grabbed his coffee and headed out the door.

At about 10:00 AM Frank got a call from his Wife Lisa.

"I saw the note to Suzy, what's that all about?"

"Have you seen her at home?" Asked Frank.

"No, I just got up. It looks like they were playing the PS3 and stepped out" said Lisa.

William Pike

"No, that's the way it was when I left for work, the girls were not home when I got up at 6:30. I think they snuck out to some boy's house or something. She gets that after you."

"No, I always made it home before my Dad got up" Lisa said joking.

"Well, Baby when she gets home have her call me. She's not eighteen for two more months, and we have rules."

"Yes sir."

"I'm not joking, I got her tickets for the oh so cool Black Eyed Peas."

"Don't be too upset."

"Listen I have to go, I'll call you at lunch, I love you and the Baby."

"We love you too."

Before Frank knew it, it was noon, he punched out for lunch and called his Wife.

"Hello."

"Hey Babe it's me, did Suzy ever call, did she come home?" asked Frank.

"No, I'm starting to worry, her friends have been blowing up her cell phone all morning."

"Yeah something's wrong, I'm calling Peyton's Dad, if he hasn't heard from them, I'm calling the Police."

"Frank the Police!"

William Pike

"Something's wrong Lisa I can feel it. I'll call you back."

"Call as soon as you talk to Tommy."

Frank always felt intimidated when he talked of Peyton's Dad. He was a big wide shouldered man, with lots of tattoos, and had a menacing look in his eyes. Although he was very polite and treated Suzy with all the love he showed for his own Daughter, he still felt a chill go through him whenever he was around. Frank watched the HBO special "Men who murder" Tommy guns Margolin and Brandon knockout Smith were two scary men. He took a deep breath and called Tommy. He let it ring and ring, but got no answer, next he called The Beach.

"The Beach, Cindy speaking."

"May I speak to Tommy Margolin please?"

"One minute please."

"Hello" Tommy answered.

"Tommy it's Suzy's Dad Frank. Have you seen or talked to Peyton or Suzy today?"

"Nope, been fishing all morning, what's up?"

"Well, when I got up this morning the girls were not home, bed was made, PS3 on pause, Suzy's purse, phone, keys, and tickets to the Black Eyed Peas were all left at home."

"Maybe they're at a friends house in the complex" said Tommy.

"Yeah that was my first thought too, but I don't know Tommy, this is not like our girls."

"No leaving without writing a note is not like Peyton, but it's a big day for the girls, they're going to the biggest concert of the year, along with most of their friends, I'm sure there at a friends house getting ready and all worked up, even this early."

"You're probably right Tommy, I just got a bad feeling is all."

"I tell you what, I'll head home and see if I got any messages from Peyton, then I'll give you a call."

"Okay Tommy, I'll talk to you then."

Frank left and walked outside of the show room where his favorite car sat, a 2010 Ford Mustang cobra, it was white with blue racing stripes down the middle, 5.0 V8 with a supercharger, putting out over 500 hp. He liked to take this car for test drives whenever he could. Today he just open the door and sat in it to think "Was Tommy right, Or was his gut feeling that was telling him something was wrong? Lisa seemed worried too…

"Fuck it!" he said out loud.

Frank picked up the phone and call the Police.

Chapter 9

KO watched Cindy mixed drinks. God she looked good in that green bikini top and short white miniskirt.

"What was that all about Tommy?" Asked KO.

"Oh that was Suzy's uptight Dad, he hasn't heard from the girls all day."

"That don't worry you?"

"Peyton's seventeen and very smart, I try not to worry too much about her."

"Here you go guys" Cindy said, as she brought their drinks.

"Cindy where is Stacy?" Tommy asked.

"Who is Stacy?"

"That new Hostess I hired the other day."

"She hasn't come in yet" said Cindy "Why does this bar need a Hostess anyway? What's a Hostess going to do?"

"Well, I can think of many, many things Stacy could do" Tommy said smiling.

"What's with you and these little short haired, hazel eyed girls anyway?"

"Nothing, I like long blonde hair, grayish blue eyes, and DD breast's too."

Cindy gave an award winning smile.

"Tommy I've worked here for four years and not once have you tried to get me into bed."

"Cindy your the hottest, and best Bartender in this whole city, with the body of a goddess I tell you, if we had sex, I would never be satisfied by another woman again. Plus KO's in love with you, and I never mess with his old ladies."

"Oh, all of a sudden" said KO "how did I get dragged into this?"

"You saying you don't love me?" Cindy said, as she leaned over the bar towards KO.

"Did you say something about wanting a raise?" KO said staring at Cindy's beautiful breasts.

They all started laughing.

"Cindy make us all three shots of sex on the beach" Tommy said "I think that's as close as we'll ever get."

"Coming right up."

Tommy was thinking about what Frank said "Was everything all right? What if Peyton came home and saw her new car?"

Cindy served the drinks.

"Who is making the toast" asked Cindy.

"KO's turn."

KO smiled at Tommy, held his glass up high, and yelled.

"Drink, Fight, Fuck!"

"Drink, Fight, Fuck!" Tommy and Cindy yelled back.

It was the toast of the Iron Cowboys, a toast to Benny.

"I'm going to run home guys" said Tommy "I need to hide Peyton's car, and I told Suzy's Dad I'd check the messages."

"Want me to come along" asked KO.

"No, you stay here and talk to your love, I'll be back and we'll have lunch."

Tommy got up and headed out the door. Getting out of her little VW Jetta was Stacy, she turned around and bent over to grab her purse. Tommy loved the way that miniskirt hugged her ass.

"Sorry I'm late Tommy."

"Better late than never."

William Pike

This made Stacy smile.

"Is that yours and KO's bikes?"

"Sure are."

"When you going to take me for a ride?" Stacy asked.

She seemed to be stripping Tommy of all his clothes with her eyes.

"I should be back in an hour, we'll talk about it then."

"I can't wait."

Tommy fired up his chopper, and Stacy stood there and watched him ride away.

"I'm going to eat that man alive" Stacy said to herself.

Chapter 10

It was 12:15 PM when Homicide Detective Jimmy Johnson showed up at the Sheriff Department. He punched his security code at the back door and went to the office he shared with Justine. She was nowhere in sight. He sat down and checked his messages, hoping Mr. Margolin had called, nope, nothing.

The Medical Examiner and Lab Techs had dropped off their reports, he opened the medical examiner's first.

Jane Doe was sixteen to eighteen years old, five foot five one hundred and five pounds. She died of strangulation, and was raped by up to five men. There were two types of semen and three types of DNA from saliva. She had bite marks on her inner thighs. It was the M.E's opinion that the rape and the bite marks were committed after she was dead. There was very little blood from the wounds on her thighs and not at all in the vagina of the victim. It was also the opinion of the M.E that two men had intercourse with the dead victim, and three had oral sex with the dead victim.

"Why would they kill her, raped her, and then have oral sex with her? What pleasure did a rapist get out of that?"

JJ was lost and without words to describe how sick these men must be. He moved on to the Forensics Lab's report.

There were five different sets of boot prints, three were unknown makes, one was made by a pair of Harley-Davidson boots, one made by a pair of Diehard boots, both size ten. The other three were sizes nine, eleven, and twelve. There were no fingerprints on any of the beer bottles, but there were prints left by leather gloves. The stain on the red and white bandanna that was found under the body of Peyton Margolin was a heavyweight motor oil, mostly used in motorcycles. The same oil was recovered from the parking lot by the tire marks. The two tire marks were that of a 180 series pirelli and a 145 series Dunlop, both left by motorcycles. The DNA recovered from the M.E and the hospital was now being ran through the DNA databank.

JJ had a very bad feeling about all this information.

"Did a biker gang rape and try to kill both these girls to get back at Tommy Guns Margolin?"

JJ had no doubt that they were bikers, and after the story Justine had told him…

"Detective Johnson line two" said the intercom.

JJ punched line two.

"Detective Johnson."

"Hey JJ, Deputy Hart up here at the front desk."

"What's up Hart?"

"I got a dad on the line named Frank Simpson. He says his 17-year-old daughter may be missing, but it's only been about six hours. I was going to have him call back later, but then he said she was with her best friend Peyton Margolin, so I put him on hold, he's on line one."

"Okay great, hey look have you seen Detective Scott?"

"Not today."

"Okay Hart, good job thanks."

"Homicide Detective Jimmy Johnson."

"Like ahhh.... the NASCAR driver?"

JJ thought Frank Simpson sounded nervous about making this call.

"Yeah except I'm black and I drive a Chrysler."

"Look I think there's a mistake I was put on hold, I didn't ask to talk to Homicide."

"Are you home Mr. Simpson?"

"No, I'm at work."

JJ always thought it best to tell the family in person, because you never know what a person might do after learning a loved one has died.

"Mr. Simpson there's been some trouble and I'm going to need you to meet me at your home A.S.A.P."

There was a long pause.

"Mr. Simpson."

"What's the trouble?"

"I really need to talk to you and Mr. Margolin, have you spoken to him at all?"

"About five minutes ago, he just got done fishing and he was at his bar."

"Okay look, what's your address?" JJ asked.

"1331 Winter Gardens."

"I'll see you there in twenty minutes, will that work for you?"

"Sure… I guess, is Suzy okay?"

"I'll see you in twenty."

JJ hung up before Mr. Simpson could ask anymore questions, then he called Justine, her cell phone rang and rang…

Chapter 11

..He was so strong and confident, Justine loved to watch him play football, she was so in love... She would wear Tommy's letterman jacket to every game, it was purple with white sleeves, and it had a big gold S on the front for Santana. She was going to tell Tommy how she felt, but he had a girlfriend, a senior, and Justine was only a sophomore, but she had to tell him, because in two months he would graduate. Tommy saw her walking towards him, they locked eyes and he smiled. This was the moment Justine had been waiting for....The school bell rang and then it rang again...

Detective Scott woke up with her heart racing and didn't know where she was, then she saw Peyton laying exactly how she was when Justine fell asleep. Justine's phone rang again, she picked it up and push the connect button.

"Detective Scott."

"Hey little lady" said JJ.

"Hey big guy, what's up?"

"Where are you at? It's 12:30" asked JJ.

"Shit… sorry JJ, I didn't want to leave Peyton all alone, and I fell asleep in the chair."

JJ thought about what Justine just said, she was calling the victim by her first name, and she was spending personal time with her, he let it go for now.

"Look JJ I know that sounded weird, and I'm sorry about snapping at you before, but you're right, I'm not okay, the job is getting to me, all the violence and the dead bodies, now this rape and murder. I know I told you about being attacked in high school, well I left out many of the details JJ, and this case has just hit real close to home for me. Every time a man kills his wife, I start to hate men a little more, every time a child is hurt by violence, it makes me not want to bring another child into this world. And the sad part is, I want to be married, and I want a baby. I just can't do this anymore JJ. I'm on my way to the Department, I'm going to talk to the Captain and turn in my badge."

Caught off guard by all this JJ had to take a minute to think.

"Listen Justine, I understand, but these girls need your help right now, their families need your help. There's some real bad guys out there who need to be caught, I need your help, help me with this case, and if you still feel the same way, I'll go to the Captain with you… look Justine, Jane Doe is Suzy Simpson, I just got off the phone with her Father, I'm on my way to talk with him, he said Mr. Margolin is at his bar The Beach, I need you to get a hold of him."

"Okay JJ you're right, I'll pull it together, but I'm done after this case."

"We'll talk about that when the time comes" said JJ "also I got the M.E and the Lab reports right here, we got a lot to go on, real solid stuff. After we talk to the next of kin, let's go over all of it."

"Okay I'll see you at the office" said Justine.

Justine hung up and looked at Peyton… poor Peyton.

"You're going to be okay Sweetie, and I'm going to get the men who did this to you, for you and for your Daddy."

While Justine walked to the gift shop she called 411 and got the number to The Beach and called.

"The Beach, Stacy speaking."

"Mr. Margolin please."

"He just stepped out, would you like to speak to Mr. Smith, or is there something I can help you with?"

"Yes, could I speak to Mr. Smith please."

"One minute please."

Stacy walked over to the main bar were Cindy was showing KO how she didn't have any tan line under her miniskirt.

"KO you got a call."

KO walked to the phone and Stacey checked out Cindy's no tan lined ass.

"Is that how you get a raise around here?" Stacy asked Cindy.

"That's one way, but don't you worry I think Tommy has big plans for you, and you'll get plenty of raises out of him."

Stacy smiled at that and licked her lips as if she was cleaning something off the sides of her mouth.

She's good, real good, Cindy thought.

"Hello."

"Mr. Smith?"

"Ahh...KO please."

"Okay KO, this is Detective Justine Scott, I need to speak to Mr. Margolin, do you know where he went, or do you have his cell phone number?"

"What's this about?"

"I'm afraid I can't tell you that."

"Well, then I'm afraid I can't help you Detective."

The last thing KO wanted to do was help the police find his friend "what the hell was going on?"

"Look KO it's an emergency, and it has to do with Peyton Margolin."

"Peyton, is she okay?"

"I can't say at this time, do you know where Tommy is or not?"

"He's on his way home and he don't have a cell phone on him."

"Okay thank you KO, I'm on my way there then, I owe you twice now."

Justine hung up and KO was confused, what did she mean about owing him twice?

At the gift shop Justine bought flowers, a balloon that said get well soon, and a card. She wrote "Stay strong Peyton, love Justine Scott" She dropped off the flowers, balloon, and card at the room, and gave Peyton a soft kiss on the cheek.

"Daddy will be here soon. You just rest for now Love."

Chapter 12

I'm alive? I'm in a Hospital… Peyton could hear people talking from time to time. She heard a man call himself Doctor Fouts, and lots of nurses would say nice things to her.

She still couldn't open her eyes, or move any part of her body, but she didn't feel any pain either, which was good.

She wished she could hear her Daddy's voice, or even uncle KO's.

She thought about her Mom, but she knew her Mom would just be mad at her, and probably say it was her own fault.

There was a nice lady named Justine, who talk to her a lot, she had a nice voice, she liked Justine. Even when it was quiet, Peyton never felt alone. She knew the nice lady Justine was always in the room with her, she could smell her perfume, it was called J-Lo, Peyton had the same perfume at home.

"Daddy will be here soon" said the nice lady Justine "you just rest for now Love."

My daddy?… that was the best news in the world to her. Then all was quiet and she could smell flowers, pretty flowers, she was sure. Peyton eased her mind and rested, just like the nice lady Justine said. Her Daddy… she couldn't wait to hear his voice...

Chapter 13

"Mr. and Mrs. Simpson?"

"Yes," Lisa and Frank said at the same time.

"May I come in? I have some news to tell you, and it might be best if we could sit. I also have some very important questions I need to ask."

"Come on in… Detective Johnson right?" Said Frank.

"That's right, thank you."

This was the part JJ hated. Maybe the job was getting to him too. He found it very difficult to tell this Father and pregnant Mother that their 17-year-old Daughter was raped and murdered, or murdered and raped as the M.E says. "Just make it simple he thought."

"Mr. and Mrs. Simpson I'm sorry to tell you that your Daughter Suzy Simpson and Peyton Margolin where the victims of a violent attack last night between 12:00 and 2:00 AM. They were attacked by what we believe to be up to five men. They were both raped, one of the girls died at the scene, the other is at Grossmont hospital in a coma. I'm sorry to tell you that Suzy is the victim that died."

Lisa and Frank Simpson just sat there, they didn't say anything. Mrs. Simpson started to cry out.

"No, no, no, no!" Then she was screaming " no! No!"

Now she was crying so hard, she was barely able to breathe, Mr. Simpson held her tight, and tears were running down his face. He locked eyes with Detective Johnson, the hurt he saw in Frank's eyes was like no other he had ever seen.

"Why?" Frank Simpson asked.

JJ felt his own eyes starting to tear up, he walked out of the condo to swallow some fresh air…

Tommy pulled into his driveway and saw Peyton's new BMW. He parked his bike and walked over to the car, opened the door and sat inside it. Tommy never even had a car this nice. But he loved Peyton more than he loved himself, and with all the A's in school, and on the way to college, she more than deserved the best. He found the keys under the seat, started the car and pulled it up to the garage. He hopped out, punched in the code to the garage door and it started to roll up. He pulled the BMW in and then closed the garage door. Tommy then went to open his front door, he found a business card on the door "Sheriff's Department Homicide Detective Jimmy Johnson."

"What the fuck!"

Tommy unlocked the door and went inside, he walked to the kitchen counter and pushed the play button on the answer machine. There were three messages, the first was from Detective Johnson, he said to call A.S.A.P. The second was from Frank Simpson, the third was from KO, it was left about ten minutes ago.

"Tommy, look there is a Detective Scott on the way to your house, she said it was about Peyton. Please call me and let me know what is going on."

Tommy's mind was racing. He dialed Peyton's cell phone number, the phone was off.

"What the fuck is going on?"

He heard a car pull up to the house. Tommy walked to the front door. A short dark-haired girl about five foot two or so was getting out of her car. She was very pretty, as she got closer, even after 20 years, Tommy knew who she was, Justine the girl he saved in the park. She looked as if she could still go to high school. He knew something was wrong, she didn't smile when she saw him.

"Tommy Margolin, I'm Detective Justine Scott."

Detective? Tommy was lost, what the hell was going on?

"I remember you Justine, always have. It's good to see you, but what's going on? KO called and said something about Peyton."

He remembers me… after all these years… God how was she going to break the news to him? Her tough Detective persona broke down and she started to cry, tears were running down her cheeks. Tommy stepped forward, just like he did twenty years ago, he held her in his arms. He kissed her softly on top of the head just like the last time he held her.

"You okay? Please tell me what's going on."

"I'm sorry Tommy, Peyton has been hurt and raped, she's at Grossmont hospital in a coma, and Suzy Simpson was murdered."

Tommy kept a hold of her, she could feel his whole body loosen, and then he fell to a sitting position. Tommy looked up at her with his beautiful eyes, they were full of tears, and Justine felt her heart break for him. He got up and walked to Justine's car and got in the passenger seat, he didn't say a word, he left his front door wide open…

Chapter 14

Tommy walked into room 312, Peyton didn't look like Peyton, she had no hair, her whole face and head were swollen, they looked ready to burst. She had tubes coming out of her head and nose. Tommy sat on the edge of the bed and held her hand.

"Baby Girl… I hope you can hear me Baby Girl, Daddy's here, and I love you, I love you so much, I'm proud of you, I'm so proud of you for being strong, I'm so sorry Baby Girl, I'm so sorry."

Tommy sat there on the bed and cried, he cried for what seemed like forever. He felt a hand on his shoulder, he looked up into the tear filled eyes of Justine. She leaned down and kissed him softly on the lips.

"She's going to be okay, she's strong, she's a Margolin" said Justine.

Justine turned and walked out of the room. Tommy held Peyton's hand and talked to her about the times they went camping, to Disneyland, and Magic Mountain.

When Tommy was in prison, his Cellmate once told him he was shot in the head and was in a coma for three months. He said the weird thing was he could hear everybody and everything going on. Tommy hoped this was true, because he wanted her to know she wasn't alone, and that she was loved.

A Nurse came in and checked all the monitors and replaced Peyton's IV bag.

"She's a tough girl, how are you holding up?"

"Not too well, I don't know what to do" said Tommy.

"Well, Honey you may not think you know what to do, but you're doing it right now. She's lucky to have a Mom and Dad like you two."

"Mom?" Tommy asked confused.

"The woman outside the room talking to the big guy, Justine is her name I believe."

"That's not her Mom" said Tommy.

"Oh….Sorry, I just assumed that she was, she has not left the Girl's side since she got here. She slept in that chair till about 12:30, the only time she left was to get you."

"I see, well she is a very good person, that's for sure."

"I would say so, you guys keep your heads up, the Doctor says she'll pull through, he'll be waking her up in four to seven days if all goes well."

"Thank you for all that you guys are doing" said Tommy.

The Nurse walked out, Tommy got off the bed and walked over to the flowers, there was a balloon that said get well soon, and a card, he opened the card and read it.

"Stay strong Peyton… Love Justine Scott."

Who was this Angel of a woman that had jumped into their lives with so much love and care? What was that kiss about? Tommy was so lost and confused, he didn't know what to think about everything. He needed to pull himself together, Peyton needed him, and he needed to find the person who did this to his Daughter.

KO got the phone call from Detective Scott, she said Tommy would like him to come to Grossmont Hospital, room 312 in the ICU, and to see if he could get in touch with Peyton's Mom Kim.

KO found her at the strip club where she worked.

"This is Kimi."

Kimi was her stage name, and KO thought it sounded Asian.

"Kim it's KO, there's been a problem and Peyton is at Grossmont hospital, room 312 in the ICU. Tommy's there now, and I'm leaving right after this call."

"Well, I'm working, I'm sure Tommy's taking care of everything" Kim said.

"Look you selfish Bitch! Tommy told me to call you, so I am, I don't like you and I never did, but Peyton's hurt, and if I don't see you down at the hospital to check on your little girl, I'll come down there and drag your skank ass off that fucking stage, throw you in the trunk and bring you myself."

KO slammed the phone down and walked out of the office. He needed to tell Cindy that she was going to have to lock up for him. When he got to the bar she was telling a joke to a group of college men.

"The Dad says, Son what would you like for your birthday?"

"I would like a new bike" says the Son.

"Son the mortgage on his house is $300,000 dollars, I'm afraid we can't afford a new bike this year."

Later that night the Boy was walking by his Parents room when he heard his Dad say "I'm pulling out!"

Then his mom said "No wait, I'm coming too!"

The next morning the Dad sees his son heading out the door with a suitcase in his hand.

"Where you going Son?"

"I heard you telling Mom you were pulling out, then she said she was coming too. I'll be damned if I'm going to stay here all by myself with a $300,000 dollar mortgage and no new bike!"

Everybody at the bar laughed except KO.

"What's up?" Cindy asked.

"Hey I got to take off, lock up for me. I don't know when I'll be back."

"Everything okay?"

"I don't think so" answered KO.

When KO showed up at the hospital he stopped at the gift shop, bought a teddy bear and some flowers. He still didn't know what had happened, but he knew Peyton was hurt.

KO took the elevator to the ICU and asked the Nurse for room 312, who pointed the way to him. There was a short dark-haired woman standing outside room 312. He knew her from somewhere, but couldn't quite figure it out. She seemed to know who he was though.

"Hi KO."

"Ahh....Detective Scott?" asked KO.

"Yes, Tommy's inside."

"Where do I know you from?"

"We went to high school together, you, Tommy, and Benny saved me in the park one night."

"Justine? Well, you're all grown up, and a Detective no less. So what's going on here?"

"Peyton is in a coma, Suzy and her were attacked, raped, and left for dead. Suzy died at the scene" said Justine.

KO looked up and Tommy was standing in the doorway to room 312, he had tears in his eyes. The last time he saw Tommy cry, and the only time he saw Tommy cry, was in the middle of the street holding their dead best friend Benny Tula…

All three of them heard the five inch heels coming down the hallway, they turned and saw Kim, a.k.a. Kimi walking towards them. She looked worse than KO and Tommy had ever seen her she could barely walk a straight line. She had on five inch heels, pink miniskirt, and a white tube top. She had a tattoo above her fake tits, that said fuck you! Across her chest. She walked right by them like they were not even there into the room. Ten-seconds later she came back out.

"Great job Dad, only five years with you and look what you've done to her. Are you going to find out who fucking did this, or are your ball still in prison where you left them?"

Tommy was about to answer when Justine snatched Kim up by the hair with the speed of a cat and drug her down the hallway to the elevator.

"What the fuck are you doing Bitch?" Yelled Kim.

The elevator door opened and Justine threw Kim into it and pushed the lobby button. She walked back to Tommy and KO, but nobody said anything, KO walked into the room.

KO sat on the bed with Peyton and tucked the teddy bear just under the blanket, leaving only the head out.

"Hey Beautiful, it's Uncle KO, how are you holding up? I'm not sure what happened to you, but I know whatever it was, it was hard on you, so I want you to do Uncle KO a favor and stay strong. We all love you, even your Mom was just here to see you, how about that? And don't tell your Dad I told you this, but you got a great big present sitting at home for you. Okay I'll give you a hint, just like at Christmas time. You never told on me before, so I trust you, okay ready? It's white, and it says BMW on it. I love you Peyton…"

KO dried his eyes and walked back out to Tommy and Justine.

One minute she was feeling great about dragging that good for nothing Bitch out of here, then the next thing she knew there were two huge angry men with tears in their eyes staring at her.

"Who the fuck did this?" Asked KO.

Justine knew it would come to this from the moment she read Peyton's ID. These two men would want revenge, and it wouldn't be strapping the man to a tree and kicking him in the balls.

"We don't know much yet" said Justine "but my Partner read the reports, he says we got some good stuff to work with. We'll catch whoever did this, just leave it to us."

"Did Peyton say anything before she was in a coma, or write anything down?" Asked Tommy.

How did he know she would write something down? Justine thought.

"Why do you ask that?" asked Justine.

"I know every Dad says this about their kids, but Peyton is really smart and brave, even in the worst of times she would think, she would get a name, number, car model, anything she could. I taught her this, even told her on Friday when she left for Suzy's. I tell her about the bad people in this world, so she'll know what to do if they try to hurt her."

It killed Justine to lie to this man who saved her, who she's loved for twenty years, but the last thing Peyton needed was her Daddy back in prison.

"I have not read the reports yet, I'll be doing that when I leave here."

"I would like to meet up with you later and go over the details with you and your Partner" said Tommy.

"Tommy… I don't think we'll be able to do that."

"What the fuck do you mean Justine?" KO yelled at her.

"I… I know what you're thinking guys, look your upset, but the last thing Peyton needs is to see you back in prison, please just let us do our jobs, will get these guys."

Tommy didn't answer, he walked back into the room and held Peyton's hand, KO sat in the chair. When Tommy looked up at Justine, the hurt she saw in his eyes was unbearable, right then she knew she would help them kill these men.

Chapter 15

It was just after 2:00 PM when Detective Justine Scott arrived at the Sheriff's Department. It was shift change and there were Deputies coming and going. Justine still had the same clothes on since 2:15 in the morning when she hurried out the door to the crime scene, white Nikes, Levi's, a white top, which was all wrinkled from sleeping in the Hospital. She didn't feel much better than she looked. She sat down and started to go over the reports. JJ had highlighted the facts that he thought were important. It didn't take her long to figure out that it was a group of five bikers. What she didn't know was who they were. She knew the key to breaking the case was the red and white bandana, and the word Nevada. After talking to Tommy, she believed Nevada could be somebody's name or maybe a license plate.

William Pike

They had no results back from the DNA they found on the victims yet. So what they had so far was five bikers who fly red and white colors. One had a motorcycle with a 180 series Pirelli back tire, and one with a 145 series Dunlop. They could've possibly been at The Spot Bar and Club, from the book of matches they found, but The Spot was not a biker bar, it was more of a hip-hop club. Maybe the matches were already at the scene Justine thought.

There was only one motorcycle club or gang that flew red and white in San Diego County, and that was the Demons of Chaos, but maybe it was just a biker that liked red and white, or just a supporter of the Demons of Chaos.

"Hey a little lady" said JJ as he walked.

He looked tired even though he got some rest and a change of clothes. He was wearing black shoes, black slacks, a white button up, and a purple tie.

"How did it go at the Simpsons?"

"It was one of the worst times of my career, the Mother is seven months pregnant, and the father was trying to hold it together for both of them. To say the least they're devastated."

"Tommy was not much better, I never seen a grown man with so much hurt in his eyes" said Justine.

There she goes again with the first names, all five years as her partner JJ never heard her refer to the victims this way.

"What do you think about the reports?" asked JJ.

"Five male bikers, maybe Demons of Chaos is my first guess. I think we need to go check out The Spot Bar and Club, and talk to the third watch gas station worker to see if anyone noticed any bikers, see if they say anything about the Demons of Chaos, then we track them down, connect them with the DNA, and put them away for life."

"No hits on the DNA yet?" Asked JJ.

"Nothing yet."

"Have you had lunch?"

"I stopped on the way in" said Justine.

"It's 4:00 PM right now, how about we go to The Spot, and then the gas station?"

"Okay you drive I'm beat."

"Sure thing Little lady."

It was a short fifteen minute drive to The Spot Bar and Club. The parking lot was pretty empty, maybe twelve cars were parked in it.

"I guess it's not much of a day crowd huh?" said Justine.

"No, not much of a biker crowd either, this might be a dead-end."

They walked into The Spot, there were only about fifteen customers, maybe twenty, two Bartenders, and a Doorman who didn't card them. Eighty percent of the customers were African-American, and Justine thought this was a long shot.

JJ showed his badge to one of the Bartenders.

"Homicide Detective Jimmy Johnson, and this is Detective Scott."

"What would you like to drink Detectives?" Was the response from the Bartender.

"Nothing thanks, we have a few questions about some customers you may have had in here last night. Did you work last night?"

"No sir, I work days, but Sam worked till closing. We try not to get involved in Police business, if you know what I mean" said the Bartender.

Justine took it as since JJ was black he would know what the Bartender was saying by "You know what I mean."

Trying to hold his temper and not drag this punk over the bar JJ raised his voice.

"Two teenage girls were raped, one was murdered, so no I don't know what you fucking mean! Whose Sam?"

Taking a step back the Bartender pointed to the office.

"Sam's in his office."

Sam was about 40 and unlike the Bartender he was white and seemed ready to help.

"Yes, how can I help you Detective?" Justine did the talking this time.

"We'll try to make this quick for you Sir, two girls were attacked, raped, and left for dead, one died and the other is in a coma. We believe it was five bikers. We found a book of matches at the scene, which is only a half-mile away, and they said The Spot Bar and Club on them. Did you have any customers that were bikers last night?"

Justine expected a "Sure didn't" or "No Ma'am this is not a biker bar" but her heart about stopped when Sam answered her.

"As a matter of fact we did have five bikers show up last night, but I wouldn't call them customers, anything but that. Two came inside the other three stayed outside on their bikes, it seemed like they just wanted to ask a question, or maybe they were looking for someone, but they never got the chance to ask. We don't allow gang colors or clothing in here, it just brings too much trouble. My bouncer told the two who stepped inside "Sorry no colors" the older of the two bikers said "Yeah we saw the sign on the door, we thought it meant no Blacks" my doorman is black along with most of my customers. I thought those two white guys were dead meat, but the younger one showed a gun in the waist of his pants and put his hand on it. Without a care in the world the older one walked through all these black men he just insulted, grabbed a book of matches off the bar, lit a smoke, and walked out. Men of brass balls I tell you."

"Do you happen to know what they were wearing" asked Justine.

Part of her wanted them to be Demons of Chaos, but for Tommy and KO's sake she didn't want them to be.

"They were all wearing mix colors of red and white, and leather vests" Sam said.

"Did you happen to read the vests? Were there any patches on them?"

Sam thought for a minute, he didn't really want this gang on his bad side" Justine sensed what Sam was thinking.

"Look Sam, I know you don't want any trouble, but we need to catch these men, Suzy Simpson, and Peyton Margolin's families deserve justice, they need your help"

"Peyton Margolin?… Tommy's Daughter?" Asked Sam.

"Yes, you know them?"

"Tommy is a local bar owner, I know him somewhat… They were Demons of Chaos, all five of them. I didn't see the back of their vests but my doorman did, and he told me who they were. If you could keep my name and place out of this that would be great."

"You've been a big help Sam, and we'll do what we can" Justine told him.

Once they were in JJ's car, they sat in the parking lot for a few minutes.

"What do you think?" Asked Justine.

"I think we just narrowed it down from hundreds of thousands to under… well, I don't know how many of these Demons there are, but it can't be that many."

"Yeah, I think we'll have these men behind bars by tomorrow night" said Justine.

Next they drove down the street to the gas station, and the crime scene. The guy working looked to be about twenty one, he had short blue hair, body piercings in his nose, eyebrows, and lip, he also had colored tattoos on both arms. Justine would bet her paycheck that he was on some kind of drug.

"Detective Scott and Johnson, are you Mark Lyman?"

"That's me, but I don't lie man, get lie-man?"

"Yeah we got it" said JJ.

"My Manager said to help anyway I can, so how can I help you?"

"Did you see two teenage girls late last night?" Asked Justine.

"Not that I remember, they got names?"

"Suzy Simpson and Peyton Margolin."

"No way man... No way, really?"

"So you know them?" Asked Justine.

"Ahh...Man, yeah I know them, they come in to buy... I mean they try to buy smokes all the time."

"You didn't see them last night?" Asked JJ.

"No man... Man!"

"What about any bikers?" Asked Justine.

"Bikers? Not in the store man, but when I left I walked out back, that's where I parked my ride, and there were a group of bikers back there man, standing around drinking, looked like maybe they were waiting for someone to meet them, but man I didn't talk to those dudes I've heard stories."

"So you know who they were then?" Asked JJ.

"Not who... But what they are man, Demons... Demons of Chaos!"

Chapter 16

"Prospect! Cut me a fucking line!"

Mad Dog had been up for three days or maybe four when he bent down and snorted a four-inch line of speed with a rolled up hundred dollar bill. Mad Dog had a mean look to him, he wore black boots, Levi's, no shirt, and his Demons of Chaos patch. He had a tattoo across his chest that said "Thank God I'm White" in one-inch letters.

"Any of you Brothers want this good for nothing Prospect to cut you out a line?"

Mad Dog always gave his Prospects a hard time, but he gave them a harder time around other members, and there were still about thirty Demons left over from the party Mad Dog and his chapter threw last night, Arizona, New Mexico, Nevada, and Texas outlasted everyone, and were still going strong Saturday afternoon.

"I'll take one" Monster said.

Monster was the Vice President of the Dallas Texas chapter.

"You heard him you good for nothing fucking Prospect" yelled Mad Dog.

Danny Boy was the "Prospect" and he just about had enough of this shit! All night he's been disrespected. He was ready for his patch, even if he needed to kill someone to get it.

"How old are you Prospect?" Asked Monster.

"Twenty four Sir."

"No your twenty" said Monster.

"No sir, I'm twenty four."

"You fucking talking back Prospect?" Said Lugnut from the Nevada chapter.

"No sir, it's just..."

"Shut the fuck up Prospect" yelled Lugnut.

"How old are you Prospect" Monster asked again.

"Ahh... twenty Sir."

"Mad Dog, Mad Dog!" Monster yelled "you got to be twenty one to prospect in this club, this Prospect just told me he's only twenty!"

"Did you tell him you're only twenty you fuck?" Yelled Mad Dog.

"No I..."

"You calling him a liar?" Asked Lugnut.

"Get the fuck out of here Prospect, you make me fucking sick! Go out to the parking lot and every time a Brother shows up you tell them you lied to the VP of Dallas."

"Yes sir."

Everybody in the clubhouse started laughing as Danny Boy the "Prospect" walked out the door.

"When you guys taken off?" Asked Mad Dog.

"Were all rolling out together, Nevada is tagging along to Arizona" said Monster "one hell of a party though Brother, I can't wait to come back."

They all hugged and shook hands as they said "Blood and honor" that was their club handshake. "Blood and honor."

Chapter 17

When Tommy woke up the clock in Peyton's room read 7:20 PM. He had fell asleep on the floor just after KO fell asleep in the chair. KO was still sleeping when Tommy stood and stretched.

Tommy looked at his little girl and stroked her arm. She still didn't look like Peyton. His heart felt like it was broke every time he saw her. How could someone beat this beautiful girls face in like this? And Suzy, happy all the time Suzy. He nicknamed her Bubbles, she was such a joy to be around, always laughing and smiling.

"Suzy we're going to miss you."

"You say something Tommy?" Asked KO as he woke up.

"No Bro, just thinking out loud, sorry."

"What time is it?"

"About 7:30."

"What are we going to do about this Tommy?"

"The only thing we can do, wait, hope the cops get a line on these guys, and then we'll pay them a visit" said Tommy "I want you to think about your family though KO, you got a Wife and Daughter at home that need you. This might get real ugly."

"I've thought about it Bro, and I'm going to do what you would do for me" Said KO "for better or worse, till death do us part, right? Or did I say that to my Wife?"

They both kind of smiled, and KO got up and gave Tommy a hug.

"I love you Brother, and always, I mean I will always be by your side."

"I love you too Bro… this is hard Brother… it's tearing me apart inside" said Tommy as a tear started running down his cheek again.

"Tommy… KO."

They let go of the hug, and standing in the doorway was Frank and Lisa Simpson.

"This a bad time?" Asked Frank.

"No, no, don't be silly" said Tommy "come in, come in."

Lisa and Frank walked into the room Lisa wore a long black dress that hugged her belly, and Frank still had his work clothes on from this morning.

"We just couldn't sit around the house anymore Tommy."

William Pike

"I can't imagine how you two are keeping it together?" said Tommy.

KO walked out of the room to give them some privacy, he didn't know what to say to anyone.

"I'm sorry Tommy" said Frank "I let this happen to our little girls, I should've heard them leave....Something..."

"Don't be foolish Frank, it's not your fault. I'm very sorry about Suzy, if there is anything I can do just ask."

Frank looked at Peyton and his Wife, when he look back at Tommy, he looked broken, lost, and alone.

"Tommy could we step outside for a minute?"

"Sure Frank."

Tommy walked over to Peyton, gave her a kiss, and said "Daddy will be right back" then he turned and gave Lisa a hug and kissed her on the forehead.

"Stay strong love, think about the Baby coming."

Tommy walked out of the room, KO was shaking Frank's hand and they all walked down the hall to where the vending machines were.

"I never told you this before Tommy, but I saw the HBO special "Men who murder" a couple of times, and I just couldn't understand how people could kill other people."

Frank looked from Tommy to KO.

"Now I understand Tommy. We need to find these men, and when we do, I need you to help me kill these Mother Fucker's, every last one!"

Tommy looked at KO, and they both looked at Frank and nodded. "They had just become three."

"We'll let you know when it's time Frank, till then keep your ears open, and see what info you can get out of the cops. Till we get some info on these men, we just have to wait" said Tommy "your Wife and Baby need you, so stay strong for them. We'll all get through this, and there will be a pile of dead rapist and child killers when it's over!"

Justine showered, put on a sweatsuit, and headed out the door, it was 7:40 PM. She grabbed the book Twilight the vampire saga, she had been wanting to read it, so she thought she would take the time and read it to Peyton.

JJ and her worked all day on the evidence they had, to try to get some warrants, but the DNA still had no matches. They needed a little more evidence to make this stick in court. All they knew was that it was five Demons of Chaos, but not which five.

Justine put the note she wrote for Tommy in her pocket. She couldn't believe what she was about to do. Her life as a cop was over, she knew she would have to quit for sure now.

When she got to room 312 it was about 8:00 PM, and the Simpsons were leaving, they didn't even give her a second glance.

William Pike

"Tommy, KO, how's it going?"

"Slow, the slowest day of my life" said Tommy "how did it go at the office?"

"Can we talk alone Tommy."

Tommy looked at KO, KO shrugged his shoulders, so Tommy stepped outside the room with Justine and walked down to the vending machines. There was a nurse buying a coke, so they waited till she was done

"Tommy I have so much I need to say to you, if you could just hear me out, just listen for a minute, I wanted to tell you this for twenty years... Tommy... I love you, I've loved you since you walked me home and kissed the top of my head, I'm still in love with you. You were there and then you were gone, the years flew by and I never saw you around, then Benny died, you went to prison, I became a cop, and now this tragic event has brought us back together. I know you have Peyton to worry about, and it's selfish for me spring this on you right now, but I need too, in case... in case something happens to you and... and I don't get the chance to tell you how I feel in my heart. I love you, and I love Peyton because she's part of you. I have something for you, it's the best I can do."

She handed him the note.

"I'm going to quit the force after this case, I don't know what I'm going to do, I just can't do this anymore. I want a family, I don't want to see any more dead people."

Tommy opened the note, there were just six words on it "Five men, all Demons of Chaos" Tommy looked up and pulled Justine into his arms, when she looked up he kissed

William Pike

her on the lips, not the way she had kissed him earlier, but he kissed her long and deep and then he looked into her eyes.

"You've just found a family, and I know that we'll both love you."

Justine smiled and cried at the same time, she hugged Tommy with all her strength.

KO was sitting on the bed talking to Peyton when they walked in, Tommy thought he heard the word BMW, but KO stopped talking when he heard them. Justine sat in the chair, and Tommy handed KO the note, KO read it, looked at Tommy, got off the bed and walked out of the room, Tommy followed, Justine said a silent prayer......

Chapter 18

"What the hell is going on Tommy?" KO asked, as they both got into his 2010 yellow Chevy SS Camaro. "I mean really, Demons of Chaos, is this a bad nightmare? I didn't even know we had Demons in San Diego!"

"I don't know KO... I never heard of Demons in San Diego, and I've never had a run-in with their gang. I don't know why they did this to Peyton and Suzy, but I'll make sure I ask them why right before I end their life's."

"What's the plan?" Asked KO.

"We need to find out all we can about these Demons of Chaos, without bringing too much heat on to us. How many there are here in "Dago", who they are, where they hang out, once we do that, we'll pay our old friend Ken Smith a visit, I'd say he owes us a favor for saving his kid this morning" Said Tommy "drop me off at my place, and then you run home and grab your bike, meet me back at my house, will run up to The Beach grab our toys out of the safe, then we'll go bar hopping and see what we can learn."

"Are we bringing the Iron Cowboys back?" Asked KO.

Tommy thought about this as KO fired up the Camaro. Should they declare war against all the Demons of Chaos, or should they hit them fast here in San Diego and leave the rest of their club wondering what the hell happened in San Diego? Tommy knew they had close to a thousand members nationwide, KO and Tommy would end up dead or in prison eventually.

"No, the Iron Cowboys stay with Benny, resting in peace" said Tommy "this is a new type of war, one that will only last a day, and nobody knowing it was us, except Justine probably and I think Frank Simpson has the right to draw blood."

"What do you think of Justine" asked KO.

"She's an Angel sent from God to help me and Peyton. She says she's loved me every since the park KO, and to tell you the truth I never forgot about her or that night, I would think about her in prison, when I needed a good laugh, I would always think about her kicking that sick fuck over and over in the balls. I don't know how it happened KO, but I think Justine is my girl now, and… and I think I'm in love for the first time in my life."

KO smiled, hit the gas pedal and they were doing 60 within 4.0 seconds.

Tommy's front door was still open when KO dropped him off, the Homicide Detective's card lay in front of it, as a cold reminder of Suzy's fate. Tommy shaved his head, face, and took a quick shower, when he opened the closet for his clothes, his Iron Cowboys patch was hanging there, and next to it a black T-shirt with the words "Drink, Fight, Fuck" across the front, it was a shirt dedicated to Benny. He knew what he told KO about not bringing the Cowboys back, but he couldn't help but put the shirt on, along with black jeans and black riding boots.

Tommy walked in to Peyton's room and to him it smelled like Justine, he couldn't put his finger on it but it definitely smelled like Justine. Soon they all three might be living in this house together, like a real family. Tommy liked the thought of that. In Peyton's room there was a bed, nightstand, dresser, and computer desk with that kid Edward from the Twilight movie on it as a screen saver, that all the girls loved, high school girls who loved Vampires, things have sure changed. On the dresser was a pitcher of Peyton and himself, it was taken five years ago when Tommy had gotten out of prison, Peyton was eleven years old, they were looking at the camera with Disneyland in the background, it was only Tommy's second day home when he took her there, just the two of them. The picture frame she bought for the picture said "The best day of my life" Tommy read it as his eyes started to water, then he heard KO's bike pull up to the house.

It was hard to smile and almost impossible to laugh, but when Tommy saw KO come through the front door they both smiled from ear to ear as they read each other shirts "Drink, Fight, Fuck" and KO's "God forgives, Cowboys Don't" the Iron Cowboys were not back… not really…

They shook hands as if they just met or maybe how you would after you sealed the deal for your first house you just bought, and without a word they fired up their choppers and headed to their club.

The parking lot was full and there was a line out the front door of about twenty people, it was only 9:30 on a Saturday night. Tommy and KO walked through the crowd to the front door, Stacy was there talking to one of the SDSU football players, she smiled at Tommy as he walked by, even though he didn't look at her. The club was packed and horny college kids were dancing all over each other. The DJ was good, he could get the feel of the crowd and before you knew it girls would be on top of the bar and the pool tables, shaking it like a salt shaker as Little John would sing it. Tommy still didn't know what that one song even meant "all skeet, skeet, Mother fucker, all skeet skeet" but the college girls loved it and the college boys loved the girls, Tommy would even catch himself singing that catchy hook on good nights.

Tonight he had no time to sing as they worked their way through the crowd like they were on a mission. Cindy was in the office doing paperwork at a desk when they walked in.

"Why are you not behind the bar?" KO asked.

"I got off at 8:00, I'm here to close for you because you asked, it seemed important, so here I am."

"Thanks" said KO.

Tommy opened the safe and pulled out two colt 45's.

"Are you guys going to tell me what's going on?" Asked Cindy.

KO was about to reply when there was a knock at the office door, Tommy put one of the 45s into his waist and threw the other to KO, then he got the door. It was Stacy and she seemed like she had been drinking.

"Hey Tommy are you still going to let me ride it, or can we do what your shirt says Drink, Fight, and Fuck?" she smiled that bad girl smiled.

"You're fired!" Said Tommy.

He slammed the door in Stacy's face.

"Okay now I know something bad is going on" said a stunned Cindy "guns are one thing, but I've never seen you turn down pussy that fine, I'm not much into girls but even I would eat that girl like it was chocolate cake."

Still not smiling Tommy said "you're like family Cindy, but it's best you don't know what's up, just know Peyton is in a coma right now, and we're going to need you more than ever around here the next few days."

"Peyton… Oh my God Tommy, I'm so sorry, anything you guys need just say it."

"You're the Boss now Cindy" said KO "open, close, you know the drill, it might only be a few days, it might be longer, just keep the bar going. Your wages just tripled and you don't have to work behind the bar anymore if you don't want to."

Trying to take in all these new responsibilities, Cindy didn't really know what to say, but she knew they would both do it for her.

"Okay, I love you guys, be safe and come back to me okay."

Full Throttle was the first biker bar on their list. They headed east on I-8, it was a nice night in San Diego about sixty five degrees in late May. They flew down the road at about eighty miles an hour with no jackets on just their shirt's blowing in the wind, with the words that meant more to them than people would know who just happened to read them. There was a passion inside KO and Tommy a passion they've had all their life, from high school football to working on their choppers, anything they loved they put a hundred percent of their heart and love into it, but all that put together didn't even come close to what was burning in their hearts tonight as they flew down the freeway with the wind in their face and their 45s tucked in their waist…

They could only see about seven bikes when they pulled into Full Throttle's half full parking lot, three women stood out front smoking, they smiled at the two six foot three tattooed bikers as they walked by them into the bar.

The Full Throttle had not changed at all in the last ten years since KO and Tommy were there last, a pool table to the right, one in the middle, a bar along the right wall, dance floor to the left, bathrooms in the back, tables and chairs throughout the rest. There were five bikers at a table to the left and two at the bar, the rest of the customers were middle-aged and the bar had a mellow feel to it, nothing like the old days. They walked to the back of the bar and took a table, sitting with their backs to the wall so they could see the whole bar. A waitress asked for their order within thirty-seconds.

"We have a special tonight for drop dead sexy men" she said with a smile, more at Tommy then KO.

"Yeah, and what would that be?" Asked Tommy.

"Too buttery nipples with me on top."

She was wearing black knee-high leather boots, a black short, short miniskirt, with a tank top that said "I like to ride hard and fast" on it.

"We'll take the shots" said Tommy "along with two red bull vodkas, and I'll think about you on top Baby, but I don't know if you'll be able to hang on."

Tommy knew he had to turn on his charm to get the information he needed, nobody was going to talk freely about the Demons of Chaos. She seemed please.

"Mmmm...Like that big guy? I'm Roxie" she said putting out her hand.

"Tommy Guns, this is my Brother KO."

Tommy shook her hand, but she brought his hand up to her mouth and put two of his fingers in it and sucked them all the way to the back of her throat.

"Mmmm....You taste good Tommy Guns" Roxie said as she walked away.

"Now that girl would be a handful" said KO.

"Did you see the five bikers at the table" asked Tommy.

"Yeah three Warlords and the other two look Independent."

"The old man looks familiar" said Tommy.

"What the fuck are those two big bastards looking at?" Said PitBull.

PitBull was the president of the Warlords San Diego chapter, he was sitting with Lucky and Heavy D who were also Warlords, the old man and his partner had just bought them a round of drinks. PitBull felt that this bar was his and the Warlords bar, even though he didn't own it, it was his spot, no other biker or club came to Full Throttle anymore without being invited by them.

"With all due respect" said the old man "them there are Iron Cowboys" the one on the left is Tommy Guns and his partner there is KO. I wouldn't go disrespecting no Iron Cowboys if I were you."

"Yeah, well your not me old man!" PitBull spit back.

"Iron Cowboys huh" said Heavy D "I think we know someone who would like to get a hold of them two, don't you Pit?"

"Yeah I would say that's an understatement."

Roxie brought back the shots and the red bull vodkas, Tommy and KO threw the shots back and Roxie sat on Tommy's lap.

"How'd you like the way those buttery nipples tasted?"

"I could think of a couple that would taste better" said Tommy "hey Roxie, you wouldn't happen to know if the Demons of Chaos come around here, or where they might hang out do you?"

Roxie looked over her shoulder at PitBull and the gang.

"Ummm... We don't talk about no Demons around here, this is the Warlord spot, talking about Demons could get a man in trouble around here, even two as big as you guys."

"Looks like that troubles on its way over" said KO.

Roxie got off Tommy and left to the women's restroom.

There were three of them, the one leading the other two was short with a square blockhead, one was fat, and the third was a youngster, they walked straight up to the table and Tommy slid his 45 out and held it under the table. The blockhead spoke first.

"You two Iron Cowboys Tommy Guns and KO?"

"That's right" answer Tommy.

"I'm PitBull, this is Heavy D and Lucky, Warlords "Dago" chapter. There's someone I know who would like to get a hold of you two."

"Is that a fact?" Said KO.

"Yes, it is" PitBull said holding out a cell phone to Tommy.

Tommy didn't take the phone, he had his 45 out and wanted his other hand free, KO took the phone from PitBull.

"This is KO."

"Mother Fucker, how the fuck have you guys been?"

KO said nothing at first as he was trying to place the voice.

"Cat got your tongue? It's Tiny Brother, mother fucking Tiny!"

"Hey tiny, what's up Brother, it's been a longtime Bro" said KO "when did you get out?"

"About a year ago. I sure missed you guys. I love you Mother Fuckers, you guys are somewhat famous with the Warlords. I got hundreds of stories about you crazy Fuckers. Put Tommy on KO."

"Sure thing Bro, come down when you get a chance it would be great to catch up."

KO handed Tommy the phone, Tommy put his 45 back in his pants and PitBull smiled with approval, like all the stories Tiny had told just now became true.

"Tiny, how you been my Brother?"

"Good, good, just drinking and fucking as much pussy as I can. Nine years I went without a cold beer and a hot pussy. What about you Tommy Guns, how's life?"

"Not too good right now" Tommy said.

Tommy got up and walked to the bathroom to get a little privacy, there were two men using the restroom and he waited for them to leave.

"Anything I can help with?" asked Tiny with concern in his voice.

"It's all bad Tiny, my little girl Peyton, the one in my pictures you saw in prison, her and her best friend were attacked, raped, and left for dead, Peyton is in a coma, her friend is dead, don't ask how I know, but it was the Demons of Chaos. I've been out of the game for a while now, I need all the info I can get."

Tommy waited while Tiny thought about what Tommy had just said.

"Give the phone to PitBull, I'll have him fill you in, leave your number with him and get mine, I'd like to come down and see you guys soon."

"I'll do that Tiny, and hey Brother thank you. I owe you twice now."

"You don't owe me shit Tommy Guns, I'm sorry to hear about your little girl."

Tommy walked back to the table, KO and the Warlords had five shots of Jack waiting, Tommy handed the phone back to PitBull who walked away with it, he came back picked up his shot and said a toast, it was a toast that gave Tommy goosebumps.

"The enemy of my enemies must therefore be my friends."

Chapter 19

Justine took a warm bucket of lightly soaped water, and with a washcloth she slowly gave Peyton a sponge bath, she wiped the dried blood away at the corners of her mouth and from under her nails, she cleaned her makeup off as best she could, she wiped down her whole body. A Nurse change the bandage on her left breast. Then Justine put a clean nightgown on Peyton, sprayed just a little J-Lo perfume on her, she hoped Peyton would like the way it smelled. Satisfied she pulled the covers up and put the teddy bear uncle KO had brought her back under the covers with just its head sticking out. Justine emptied the bucket and washed her hands, then she sat down and read Twilight to Peyton. She fell asleep right as the weird kid with some kind of superpower saved Bella from getting hit by a van...

Chapter 20

Tommy and KO followed the Warlords out to Lakeside, to a house just off Highway 67, there were no streetlights and they turned down a dirt road, after a half-mile they were at the PitBull's place. It was a ran down old house that needed paint and the lawn cut, there were two pit bulls tearing at a football. Inside was not much better, but it had a pool table, big-screen TV, a wet bar, the dining room had a large table and they all sat down while Lucky grabbed some Bud Lights.

"I'll start at the beginning" said PitBull "I'll tell you all I know, so there won't be any need to ask me any questions after I'm done. Tiny says to tell you what I know, I don't want to know why you want this and I don't want to know what you're going to do with it, and this meeting never happened, agreed?"

"Agreed" said KO and Tommy.

"Mad Dog… Mad Dog is the President of the San Diego Demons of Chaos, he prospected in prison, where he did eight out of fourteen years for rape. He would give girls GHB, that date rape drug and have his way with them, he was only convicted of one count of rape, but was suspected of many more. It's said he killed two blacks in prison, and has a tattoo across his chest that says "Thank God I'm White" you can also spot him by his patches. The Demons of Chaos have patches they can earn through doing different shit for the club. Mad Dog has a red cross on his left front side, which I hear is what you get for killing for the club. He also has white and brown wings on the left side. The Demons have white, brown, red, green, and purple wings. The way they earn their wings is the same as most outlaw clubs, but in case you don't know I'll lay it out for you.

It's called a wing party. You get a girl to let two officers of the club fuck them, both officers cum inside and on the bitches pussy, then one by one the other club members eat that cum out of the girl, for three minutes each. That's how you earn your white wings, for the Brown, red, green, and purple it's the same process, only for the brown wings it's in her ass, for red it's on her period while she's bleeding, green is if she has a STD, the purple wings are if she is dead while they do it. I've seen them all but only a handful of purple ones. Anyway Mad Dog has white and brown, he's a sick fuck.

He got out of prison two years ago and started the San Diego chapter, as of right now they only have five members and one Prospect. The Prospect is Danny Boy, the VP is Hitman, then they got Joker, Reaper, and Face. Hitman has a red cross, so we assume he's killed, Face has a large scar on his face, they have not been around that long and I don't know much about them, but they've all done time. They hang out at the Little Pub in East County and they got a clubhouse, it's an old restaurant Mad Dogs Dad left him when he passed, it's on Broadway right cross from the Tattoo Shop, you can't miss it. For a while they would be there every Sunday night, we figure that's their weekly meeting time. But all's been quiet with our two clubs so we have not checked on them lately. They're a tough bunch and they got a lot of backup all through California and fourteen other states. That's about all I got for you, I know it's not much, but I hope it helps " Said PitBull "Tiny's my uncle and he's got a lot of love for you two, if there's anything you need, You know where to find us"

"You've done more than enough PitBull" said Tommy "we'll be on our way, thank you."

They all shook hands, Tommy and KO Road off.

"What do you think?" Asked Heavy D.

"I think that the Demons won't be in Dago much longer…."

Chapter 21

Tommy stood at the door to room 312, Peyton lay the same way she had been before he left, except she had on a fresh nightgown and someone had cleaned her up. The room had the same smell as Peyton's bedroom, it was a good smell, one he was beginning to love. Justine sat in the chair asleep with a book in her lap. She had stayed the whole night with his little girl, his heart went out to this woman, this Angel sent to him. Tommy walked over to Peyton and gave her a kiss.

"Daddy's back, I love you."

Then he went over to Justine, bent down and kissed her short dark hair, she woke up and looked at him with those lovely hazel eyes, she was so beautiful, even in the morning he thought, even with squinted puffy eyes.

"Good morning Angel."

"Hey you... Good morning."

Tommy kissed her soft on the lips.

"What time you have to be at work?" asked Tommy.

"What time is it?"

"8:00 AM, they wouldn't let me in the hospital till 8:00."

"I better get going, I got a lot of paperwork to do" she said "how was your night... never mind, don't tell me a thing."

She got up and put her book on the nightstand, said goodbye to Peyton, gave Tommy one more kiss as he sat in the chair she got out of.

"Will you call me at 12:00?" Tommy asked.

"Sure Baby anything you want, just get some rest, you look beat up this morning."

"Thank you Angel... I love you..."

"I love you too" said Justine with a smile.

Chapter 22

Detective Jimmy Johnson and Justine Scott both got to the department about 10:00 AM Sunday morning. JJ thought Justine looked well rested today and it was good to see her in an upbeat mood.

"What are you working on little lady?"

"I got the profiles on the San Diego Demons of Chaos, that I sent for last night"

"Any news on the DNA?" Asked JJ.

"Don't know, could you check it out while I go over this?"

I'll do that as we speak."

JJ picked up the phone and called his buddy where they do all the DNA, Justine dug into the profile reports. There were only six profiles, five full members and one prospect, it was all adding up...

Name: David Lee Tobin, a.k.a. Mad Dog.

Gang: Demons of Chaos, President, San Diego chapter.

Description: Height, five foot ten, Weight, one hundred and ninety five pounds, Hair, brown, Eyes brown, Age, 42

California drivers license number: C560459

Address 839 Grape Street, San Diego, CA 92021.

Arrest history: Served eight years for rape, six months for battery.

Comments: Drug of choice speed, very violent temper, presumed armed and dangerous.

Name: William J. Corbin, a.k.a. Hitman

Gang: Demons of Chaos, Vice President, San Diego chapter.

Description: Age 45, Weight, two hundred pounds, Height six foot two, Hair, Brown, Eyes, Hazel.

California drivers license number: A4599621

Address: 1391 Ramo Ln., San Diego, CA 92115

Arrest history: Eleven years for manslaughter, battery with GBI, and domestic violence.

Comments: Subject is not mentally stable, drug of choice is cocaine and speed. Presumed armed and dangerous.

Name: James Hamilton Roper, a.k.a. Joker

Gang: Demons of Chaos, Sgt. of arms San Diego chapter

Description: Age, 31, Height, five foot ten, Weight, one hundred and eighty five pounds, Hair, brown, Eyes, green

California drivers license number: B4995570

Address: 2110 Front St., San Diego, CA 93112

Arrest history: no felonies.

Comments: Served in the Navy as a seal, expert in hand-to-hand combat and specialist in weapons. Presumed armed and dangerous.

Name:Larry Lee Webster, a.k.a. reaper

Gang: Demons of Chaos, Soldier San Diego chapter

Description: Age, 25, Height, six foot, Weight, two hundred and ten pounds, Hair, brown, Eyes, blue

California drivers license number: B9238410

Arrest history: Possession of a loaded firearm, 6 months.

Comments: Known drug dealer of cocaine and speed, presumed armed and dangerous.

Name: Ricky James Fisher, a.k.a. Face

Gang: Demons of Chaos, Soldier San Diego chapter

Description: Age, 30, Height, five foot nine, Weight, one hundred and eighty pounds, Hair, blonde, Eyes, blue

California drivers license number: B3359550

Address: 776 3rd St., San Diego, CA 92021

Arrest history: 6 counts of domestic violence, probation, 6 months, one year, 16 months, 32 months, 32 months.

Comments: Heavy drug user, speed, likes to beat and rape his woman. Presumed armed and dangerous.

Name: Danny Earl Lane, a.k.a. Danny Boy

Gang: Demons of Chaos, Prospect San Diego chapter

Description: Age, 24, Height, six foot, Weight, one hundred and ninety eight pounds, Hair, brown, Eyes, blue

California drivers license number: D3345560

Address: 3642 William St., San Diego, CA 93112

Arrest history: 2 years for drug trafficking.

Comments: Presumed armed and dangerous.

"These guys sure seem to fit the crime JJ."

William Pike

JJ held up his finger, he was still on the phone.

These guys made Justine sick to her stomach, their profile pictures all looked evil and she could picture them raping those poor girls, she needed a warrant, without the DNA that was going to be tough.

"No DNA match" said JJ "and I just got off the phone with traffic, this might be another break for us, the gas station on the corner of Pepper Street and Winter Gardens has a traffic camera in the intersection, they're working on getting us pictures from 12:00 AM to 2:15 AM."

"It would be nice to get a picture, anything to get the warrants would be nice" said Justine.

"What did you come up with in the profiles?" Asked JJ.

"They're all violent and a couple are rapists, they fit, it's them JJ, it's them...

Chapter 23

"Oh Daddy I love you so much" said Peyton, As she ran and jumped into Tommy's arms.

"I can't believe you got me new BMW, and it's white, it's so beautiful."

Peyton's hair had grown back and she didn't have a mark on her face, she smelled beautiful as she hugged her Daddy.

"Can we drive it Daddy, please! Let's go right now!" she begged.

"Justine can come too, we could drive out to Sunset Cliffs, it will be amazing Daddy, please!"

Peyton was so happy as she ran around her new BMW looking at it, taking it all in, it was really hers...

Tommy woke up to the phone ringing, he looked at the clock, it read 11:30 AM.

"Justine?"

"It's KO, I tracked down Ken" said KO "he's living in East County, I gave him a call and he's expecting us."

"Okay, can you come by and grab me?"

"I'm already on the highway, I should be there in ten minutes."

"Okay Bro, good work."

Tommy got up and looked at his little girl, she still didn't have hair and she wasn't happy running around her new white BMW... and Suzy would never even get to ride in it, poor Suzy, these girls deserved so much better than this. Tommy picked up the phone and called Frank...

Frank Simpson, had not slept since he got up Saturday morning, and he still had his same work clothes on as he sat on Suzy's bed. He was trying to be strong for Lisa and the Baby they would have in two months, but when she would go somewhere or fall asleep, Frank would grab of one of Suzy pillows and cry, he would cry like he never had in his life. He was so sad, and so angry that Suzy was dead. Tommy and KO were going to help him, when he thought about what they would do to these men it made him smile, it was the only thing that made him smile. Frank picked up a picture of Suzy and Peyton "Best Friends Forever" it said... Frank was pulled out of his daydream when his cell phone rang.

"Hello."

Tommy thought Frank sounded a little slow, maybe drunk.

"Frank it's Tommy, how you holding up?"

"Not too good, I haven't slept since I woke up Saturday."

"You still want blood Frank?" Said Tommy.

"You better fucking believe it!" Frank said with a start.

"Well, we got a line on them Frank, and their life's blood will all be spilt" said Tommy "I need you to do a couple things for us."

"Name it."

"We need a van, one with no windows in the back" said Tommy "so it looks as though you're just in it, rent one, borrow one, steal it, I don't care. Go buy a pizza or two, and buy a shirt from the same pizza shop if you can, after you do all this meet us at The Beach."

"Okay Tommy whatever you need."

"Get some sleep Frank, you'll do us no good if you're not rested."

Tommy hung up, Frank put the picture down he was holding on the dresser, he laid down on Suzy's bed and fell asleep within moments...

Ken Smith was ex-Army Special Forces, he loved guns and explosives. After leaving the Army he kept his love for them, but the law didn't agree to Ken's fully automatics and homemade bombs. He had been imprisoned three times for possession of firearms and sales, he had just gotten out again, and he promised his Wife it would be the last time...

Now he sat in his garage staring at all the stuff he loved with the door closed. He started to pull out all the good stuff, that he knew Tommy and KO loved.

He could hear his Son Kenny and Tank out front cleaning the fish they had caught this morning. Ken thought he was having a flashback from his time in Desert Storm when he heard noises this morning at about 4:00 AM, when he looked out the window, there were two figures in all camouflage, he threw himself to the floor and peeked out the window, the two figures walked away with fishing poles their hands.

KO pick Tommy up in the SS Camaro and they drove to Kens in a peaceful silence, when they pulled into the driveway they saw Kenny and Tank in camouflage cleaning their fishing gear and a couple Bass, they looked like Tommy and KO twenty years ago and it made them both smile.

"Sick car!" Said Kenny.

"It sure is" said KO "0 to 60 mph in four seconds."

Kenny and Tank checked out the car as Tommy and KO got out.

"Hey Tommy you got a car like this?" Asked Kenny.

"No, but I just bought Peyton a 2010 BMW 535."

"That's like a $50,000 dollar car" said Tank.

"You boys got a drivers license yet?" Asked KO.

"Yes, sir we both do."

KO thought of the numbers in his head, ten.

"Pick a number between one and ten" KO he told them.

"Ahh...seven" said Kenny.

"Four" said Tank.

KO threw the keys to the yellow 2010 SS Camaro to Kenny.

"Wash that fish off your hands and take his baby for a ride" said KO.

"Are you fucking kidding us" said Kenny.

"Be back in... Let's say 45 minutes" said KO.

"Right on."

"Cool man!"

The boys ran off to wash, and Tommy looked at KO, who loves that car more than his Wife, KO just shrugged his shoulders, Tommy shook his head and knocked on the garage door.

The door rolled up and there old friend Ken stood there in flip-flops, swimming shorts, and no shirt, he still wore his dog tags. Kenny and Tank ran by and jumped into KO's Camaro.

"Hey, what the fuck are you kids doing? Get out of that man's car!" yelled Ken.

The motor fired up and his Son back it out of the driveway.

"I think you've just been carjacked" said Ken "it's that fucking video game Grand Theft Auto I tell you, it's ruining our kids."

"I let them take it Ken" said KO.

Ken gave KO an odd look.

"Come on in and tell me what you need. By the way I heard what you did for Kenny and Tank yesterday, thanks."

They closed the door and Tommy was all business.

"I need three sawed off pistol grip 12gauge shotguns" said Tommy "with slugs for ammo, not that bird shot, we want to be able to kill an elephant. I also need a hand gun with a silencer, and last but not least a pipe bomb like the one you made for us last time for the rest stop. I need it smaller maybe eight to ten inches one to two inches around, but I want it more powerful than the last one."

"Smaller but more powerful?" Ken said "that's going to take some plastic explosives" I can do that without a pipe bomb."

"No Ken, I want it in a pipe bomb."

"Okay guys, go inside and grab a cold beer, I'll get to work" said Ken "if my Wife comes home run back in here like you just got caught breaking in."

William Pike

"I take it you got a plan?" said KO.

"Yeah, we take them at the clubhouse tonight if they all show up. I got Frank getting a van, he's going to meet us at 6:00 PM, we'll stake out the clubhouse till they're all there or most of them, and will kill them all dead, real dead."

"The Prospect might be out front, Prospects aren't allowed in meetings" said KO.

"I thought about that and I got a plan, that's why I got the silencer. The clubhouse is on the corner of Broadway and Boston Street, the next closest building is across the street maybe eighty yards, so will be okay once inside."

KO took a drink of his beer.

"12 gauge slugs, plastic explosives, I think people will hear us for a half mile."

Tommy smiled.

"We'll be long gone by then Bro."

A tan van pulled in the driveway and they ran like two kids getting caught drinking beer. Ken must've heard his Wife, because they didn't even make it to the garage door before he came running in the house, grabbed a beer and ran out the sliding glass door, kicked off his flip-flops and jumped into the pool.

When Page came outside, Ken was laying on a floaty, Tommy and KO were in chairs.

"Hey Babe" said Ken with a guilty smile "you remember Tommy and KO?"

She didn't answer the question, instead she said.

"I just saw the weirdest thing coming home, there was this brand-new yellow Camaro, you know like the one on Transformers that new movie, anyway a motorcycle cop had it pulled over, and the Boy who got out looked just like Kenny, but I think it was some private in the Army."

Ken and Tommy looked at KO and they all started to laugh…

Justine went over to the Gang unit to talk to her old Sgt., while JJ went to get the traffic pictures.

Rich Nelson, was the best when it came to information about gangs, Justine was hoping she could get some dirt from Nelson, so they could arrest the Demons of Chaos on something, just so she could get their DNA and connect them to Peyton and Suzy.

"Hey Nelson."

"Hey Justine, we've missed you around here, how is it over at Homicide?"

"To tell you the truth, I'd rather still be here" said Justine "have you heard about the two teenage girls, raped and murdered Friday night?" Asked Justine.

"I heard something about it, you thinking it's got a gang connection? Said Sgt. Nelson.

"I know it is Nelson, I just don't have enough for a warrant yet, we have witnesses who put the gang at the crime scene, we got DNA with no matches yet. I got the profiles on the Demons of Chaos San Diego chapter and they fit. I was hoping maybe you guys had something on them that you're sitting on, so we could pick them up and get some DNA."

Sgt. Nelson gave Justine a look of defeat and then broke the news that would ruin her day.

"I think maybe you're barking up the wrong tree here Justine, the San Diego Demons of Chaos hosted a party Friday night starting at 8:00 PM, it went on till Saturday afternoon, we were parked outside the club house all night keeping an eye on things. We estimate about one hundred and fifty Demons of Chaos members showed up from all over. It might've been the Demons of Chaos, but it sure wasn't the San Diego chapter."

Justine's heart stopped, not San Diego… she looked up at the clock 12:15, Tommy… I've got to call Tommy… She walked out of the gang unit without a word and went to her office.

She called room 312… no answer, she called the Nurses station on the third floor.

"Third floor Susan speaking."

"This is Homicide Detective Justine Scott, could you check room 312 for Mr. Margolin?"

"Well, Ma'am he left about twenty minutes ago with another big guy."

Justine could hear her heart beating.

William Pike

"Are you still there Detective?"

"Yes, yes thank you, how is Peyton Margolin doing?"

"The swelling is starting to go down, which is a good sign" said Susan.

"That's good news, look if Mr. Margolin comes back could you have him call me A.S.A.P?"

"I'll leave him a message, did you find the men responsible for this yet?...."

Justine hung up the phone, not San Diego chapter...
Hundred and fifty Demons of Chaos in town... Nevada, Nevada, Peyton wrote fucking Nevada in her own blood.

JJ walked in "I got the pictures, I think were going to need new profiles. He threw the pictures on Justine's desk, they were blown up to eight by tens, there were five bikers riding through the intersection of Pepper and Winter Gardens, they all had patches on, that said Demons of Chaos across the top, a picture of a demon on a chopper riding out of fire in the middle, and across the bottom it said Nevada!

Chapter 24

Tommy and KO got to The Beach about 5:30 PM, business was a little slow but it would pick up around 7:00 and the volleyball tournament which would start at 8:00 would fill the place. Cindy was behind the main bar, wearing a blue bikini and her white miniskirt, she waved but they didn't stop to chat, they walked to the office carrying the black duffel bag they got from Kens.

Frank showed up at 5:45 with two pizzas and a Pizza Hut shirt.

"They really play volleyball in here?" Frank asked.

"Yep, it's a big event around here" said KO.

"Here's the plan guys" said Tommy.

By 6:30 PM they were parked in a gray cargo van across and just down the street from the Demons of Chaos clubhouse, Tommy and KO were in the back.and Frank was in the driver seat with the Pizza Hut shirt on and two pizzas in the passenger seat, on his lap was a 9 mm with a silencer on it.

"Put this in the waste of your pants" said Tommy holding the pipe bomb out to KO.

"Fuck you, I'm not putting that bomb next to my Frank and Beans!" said KO "you put it down your pants, I'll carry mine and Frank's shotguns."

"It's got a two foot fuse, what are you scared of?" Asked Tommy.

"I don't give a fuck if the fuse is five feet, there's gun powder and C-4 in that fucking thing and I don't want it next to my Hotdog."

"What's with you calling your Dick Frank and Beans and Hot dog?" Asked Tommy.

"It's a long story" said KO "let's just say they're my Wife's favorite foods."

"There's one guys" said Frank.

It was 7:00 PM when the Prospect showed up, he got off his bike and stood next to the front door like a guard. He had his patch on, but he only had the bottom rocker that said California, he still needed to earn the center patch and the Demons of Chaos top rocker. They all stared at the Prospect and they knew he would never live to see that day come.

William Pike

At 7:25 they heard two more bikes pull up. They guessed it was Mad Dog and maybe the VP Hitman, they both had their patches on and Mad Dog unlocked the front door, they both went inside leaving the Prospect out front. They park their bikes in front of the door under the drive-through carport, which was probably used for valet parking when the place used to be a restaurant.

The sun was down by 8:00 PM when the rest of the gang showed up, they parked under the carport and went inside. Frank picked up his 9 mm.

"Not yet" said Tommy "we give them a little time to get their meeting going, that way there all in one room."

At 8:30 PM Frank pulled into the parking lot. The Prospect looked over at him as he jumped out and grabbed the two pizzas, holding the 9 mm under the boxes in his right hand, he walked up to the Prospect under the carport.

"Who ordered…." The Prospect tried to say.

Frank shot him three times in the heart, Tommy and KO were out of the van within seconds, Frank threw the pizzas down and grabbed his shotgun from KO.

They opened the front door, it led into a waiting area where there still was a Host counter, to the right was the men's and women's restrooms. Tommy held the door open as KO dragged the Prospect in from outside. Tommy led the way, with KO behind and Frank after him.

The main room was empty, to the left were couches, chairs, a big-screen TV, in the middle a pool table stood, along the wall a bar. The next room had doubled wood doors that were closed, on the door it said Demons of Chaos Members Only.

Tommy looked at KO and Frank they both held their shotguns at the ready, just like Tommy, they both gave him the nod that they were ready. Tommy took a deep breath and let it out slow. What happened next was something that you only read in a fiction book by James Patterson or maybe a Dean Koontz.

Tommy kicked the doors open and that three step through, all that Demons of Chaos were sitting in chairs in a ten foot circle, one jumped up out of his chair

"What the..."

"Boom!"

Tommy let his shotgun cut loose, it put a hole the size of a baseball in the big Demons chest, blood, guts, and pieces of backbone flew all over his Demons of Chaos Brothers and splattered across the wall. A second Demon pulled a gun, KO pulled his trigger.

"Boom!"

His shotgun exploded taking the top of the Demons head off from his nose up, brains flew up and hit the ceiling fan, as it spun it through brains here and there.

"Okay, okay... What the fuck!" yelled one of the Demons.

They all stayed in their seats with their hands held high.

"Who's Mad Dog?" Asked Tommy.

Nobody answered and Frank walked to the closest Demon and put his shotgun against his forehead.

"I'm only going to ask my questions one time, you don't answer you die" Tommy said in a cold mellow voice.

They knew he meant it.

"I'm Mad Dog" said the one to the right.

Tommy looked at him and stopped himself from pulling the trigger. It was Mad Dog with his red cross and white and brown wings, a murderer and rapist, Tommy hit him with the stock of his shotgun and Mad Dog was out cold.

Tommy looked at the other two, he asked the one that Frank had his shotgun on the first question.

"You like to rape and kill little girls you fuck?"

"What the fuck are you talking about?"

"Boom!"

Frank shotgun yelled and the Demons face and head were gone, but his arms and hands were still moving.

"Boom!"

Frank shot him again in the chest. The last Demon of Chaos sitting in his chair still had his hands up and he was sweating like he just ran around the block. KO put his shotgun in the Demons mouth.

"Open wide you fucking piece of shit!" Said KO.

"What about you, you like to rape little girls?" Asked Tommy.

Reaper knew there was no good answer to this question, if he said no he was dead, if it was yes he was dead, his Brothers lay all around him, blood, brains, and pieces of bone were everywhere, it smelled like shit and piss from their bowels releasing, he looked at Tommy.

"Fuck you!"

KO took the barrel of his shotgun out of the Demons mouth so they could understand him a little better.

"What did you say?" Asked Tommy.

"I said fuck you!"

"Boom!"

KO fired, more brains hit the wall. To Frank it look like a beautiful painting, one you might see at an art gallery, he wished he could take a picture and frame it for his wall at home.

   When Mad Dog woke up his hands were duct taped behind his back, and his feet were also taped together, he was bent over the pool table in the main room. The three men who just killed his Brothers were sitting on the couch drinking his cold Bud lights.

"Welcome back" said Tommy "it's your lucky day, you get to answer more than one question."

"Fuck you punk!" Said Mad Dog.

William Pike

Tommy got up, but KO and Frank just sat and drank their beer, the best tasting beer Frank ever had.

"You like to rape little girls?"

"Fuck you."

"Tommy walked behind Mad Dog and with both hands ripped down Mad Dogs pants to his ankles.

"What the fuck... What the fuck are you doing?" Yelled Mad Dog.

"Do you like to rape little girls?" Yelled Tommy.

"Okay, okay I raped some girls... Fuck man... That was years ago."

"What about Friday night?" Said Tommy "when you killed and raped two teenage girls."

"What the fuck are you talking about man? I was here all night man, I didn't rape no one."

"Friday night you raped two girls with four of your Brothers" said Tommy.

He stepped behind Mad Dog bent over the pool table with his pants down, KO got up and held Mad Dogs upper body as Tommy got behind Mad Dog.

"This is what happens to rapist" said Tommy reaching into his pants.

"No man please... What the fuck are you doing man... Come on... Don't... Listen, listen there were hundreds of

William Pike

Demons in town Friday. I had a party, fuck I swear" said Mad Dog "Oh fuck, oh fuck!" yelled Mad Dog.

Tommy pulled the ten inch pipe bomb out of his pants.

"Last chance to confess your sins, before I put something in your ass" Tommy said from behind.

"Okay man, okay... Fuck!"

Tommy spit on Mad Dog ass.

"No, no, Fuck ahh..."

Mad Dog sounded just like a mad dog as Tommy shoved the pipe bomb up Mad Dog's ass.

"Oh my God... Fuck, ahhh Fuck!"

KO held Mad Dog in place, Tommy took out a blue Bic lighter and lit the two foot fuse.

They left Mad Dog there screaming. They got about a block away when they heard and felt the blast.

"Anybody want some of this pizza?" Frank asked with an ear-to-ear smile...

William Pike

Chapter 25

Lugnut and the Sin City Las Vegas chapter road out of San Diego with Arizona, New Mexico, and Texas chapter. This wasn't their plan, but after earning their purple wings Friday night they needed to go see the Mother chapter of the Demons of Chaos, only the National President can give out awarded patches, and the Mother chapter was in Scottsdale Arizona.

Lugnut, Romeo, Skin, Turk, and Dave were all in the Sin City chapter and they all had their white, brown, red, green, and now they had their purple wings. They thought it was the best thing in the world, when other members of their club would see all the wings they had.

The Sin city chapter were all ages between twenty two and twenty six, one of the youngest chapters in the whole club, they were sick and twisted, other Demons would say, and they all loved to hear it. They had got their new purple wings and had them put on their vest right away, then they went to celebrate. Now they were at Hells kitchen

Steakhouse and Nude Club. It was one of the few clubs where you could eat the best steak and watch nude women. It was owned by Tom the Demons of Chaos Phoenix chapter President, and tonight everything was on the house for the Sin City boys.

"Where are we headed after the here Lugnut?" asked Skin.

Skin was the VP for Sin City, born and raised in Orange County, he was a skinhead till he was twenty one, then he moved to Las Vegas where he met Lugnut and became a Demon. He still had a shaved head and he had a big 88 tattoo on the back of it for Hail Hitler.

"I say we go visit Palm Springs chapter and party for a day or two, it's bike week in Palm Springs right now" said Lugnut "it should be a good time."

A stripper walked up to the table and sat on Romeo's lap, Romeo was young and the ladies thought he was good looking with his shoulder length hair and his bright white smile.

"Would you like a dance cutie?" Said the stripper "it's on the house, and if you're still hungry I got something you can eat."

All the Demons laughed and the long black haired stripper pulled Romeo to the VIP room. She sat him down in a private booth and began to give Romeo a lap dance, soon she was topless and on top of Romeo. She stood on the chair over his head, Romeo looked up between her legs as she pulled her white panties to the side and lowered herself onto his face.

"Yeah eat it, eat it" she said.

William Pike

She threw her head back with pleasure.

"I'm going outside for a smoke" said skin.

"Alright I'll be out in a minute" replied Lugnut.

Dave and Turk were running around the club somewhere and Lugnut got up to find them.

Skin walked outside and he couldn't believe what he saw, some fucking black bastard was sitting on his bike.

"What the fuck do you think you're doing you fucking black mother fucker!" yelled skin.

The black man was sitting on the chopper while his two friends took pictures, he got off the bike and retreated to his friends.

"Take it easy man, we were just taking a picture."

"Take it easy!" Said Skin walking towards the three men. "Take it easy, I come out for a smoke and there's some mother fucker on my bike."

"It was no big deal man" they pleaded.

Still walking towards them Skin pulled out his 357 Magnum and shot the black man in the head, blood splattered all over his two friends and they took off running, Skin fired all six shots and he hit both men, but they kept on running.

"What the fuck did you do?" Yelled Lugnut just outside the front door.

William Pike

"This fucker was sitting on my bike Bro" said Skin in defense.

"Our Brother owns this fucking place, you stupid fuck, what do you think's going to happen now?" Said Lugnut.

"I wasn't thinking about that Bro... Sorry."

"Go get the guys, we need to get the fuck out of here!"

Skin went back inside to round up the guys.

"Time to go!"

"What?" Said Dave "why?"

"There is a dead black piece of shit outside and Lugnut is having a shit fit over it."

They all got up and high tailed it out of their.

Chapter 26

While Justine drove to the hospital, she thought about the devastation that she just saw at what used to be the Demons of Chaos clubhouse, there were pieces of the building everywhere. The guys that worked at the tattoo shop across the street brought over two pool balls that flew through their window. The fire department said it was most likely C-4 or some kind of plastic explosive, a lot of it, they found one head in the bushes some fifty feet away, and two hands duct taped together in the street on Broadway. There were six motorcycles scattered across the parking lot, so they were looking for at least six bodies or body parts for six, they told her it could take a couple of days.

Channel 8 news crew showed up and Justine gave JJ a hug and told him sorry she just couldn't do this job anymore. JJ had asked her when she first arrived on the scene a couple questions.

"What are the odds of this Happening two days after the rape of Mr. Margolin's Daughter?"

Justine never answered his question, he returned her hug but didn't say anything to her as she walked to her car.

She drove to the Sheriff's Department, wrote a letter, and walked to the Captain's office, she left her badge and the letter on the desk. On the way out she took two photos out of her report, one was of the Nevada Chapter riding through the intersection, the other was of Peyton's left arm.

She knew Tommy and KO did this, but she didn't know for sure, she messed up big time and six men were dead, six men the world could do without, but still the wrong men. How would Tommy take this news, would he be upset? She thought he would be, it was 9:50, the bomb went off at 8:20, would he be at the hospital?

She got a ticket and parked underground and went to the third floor, when she got to Peyton's room Tommy was sitting in the chair reading her book Twilight out loud to Peyton.

"Hey how's it going?" She asked.

Tommy looked up and smiled.

"I'm only on chapter six, but this weird girl Bella is in love with this weird kid Edward, and something just ain't right about this story."

Justine gave a little laugh, how could this man blowup six people and then come read to his Daughter? She looked at Peyton and took the question back. She walked over and sat across his lap, she put her arms around his neck and kissed him, he pulled back.

"Did you know that you and Peyton smell the same all the time?"

Justine smiled.

"And so does Jennifer Lopez" she said "it's called J-Lo, it's a perfume silly."

"Well, all three of you smell good then."

"I have something I have to show you Tommy... First I want to tell you that I love you... And I'm... I'm sorry."

She reached into her purse and pulled out the two photos.

"I made a mistake Tommy, I tried to call, how come you never carry your cell phone?" She said lamely.

Tommy looked at the photos and he knew he killed the wrong men, he didn't feel bad about it, he knew what kind of men they were, but the burden he had lifted just fell back onto his shoulders. He put the pictures down.

"Shit happens" he said, and kissed her again.

"I quit my job too" Justine said.

He looked at her surprised

"You did?"

"Yes, I don't know what I'm going to do now."

She had the start of tears in her eyes.

"Well, I bet you'll look great in a bikini and a miniskirt, I got a Hostess position open at The Beach."

William Pike

She smiled and smacked his shoulder. He kissed her again.

"We'll worry about that when I get back from Las Vegas"
said Tommy.

Chapter 27

Billy Jean, a.k.a. Wild Bill was a member of the Demons of Chaos Phoenix chapter for the last year and a half. Wild Bill was also an undercover Alcohol Tobacco and Firearms Agent, also known as the ATF.

The Demons of Chaos were established in 1975 by Derek Ronald Stone, a.k.a. Stone, in Scottsdale Arizona. Stone died in 1997 at the age of fifty seven from multiple bullet wounds, fired by a rival outlaw biker gang. Dead by fifty seven, but not before the Demons had grew 750 members strong in ten states and Canada, now they had fourteen states and over 1000 members nationwide, that the ATF knew about. The Demons of Chaos where a criminal organization, they were involved in drugs, guns, stolen motorcycles, murder, Rape, and were in ongoing wars with at least five other major outlaw motorcycle gangs. They were spreading terror all across the United States. Although the law enforcement said that the outlaw bikers only made up for 1% of all bikers enthusiasts, they were a great danger to the people of the United States, most citizens called outlaw bikers one percenters and were scared to death of them. The United States government stepped in about twelve years ago and started their own war against the Demons of Chaos, using FBI, ATF, DEA, and local law enforcement, it was a long slow war that the Demons of Chaos were still winning.

Wild Bill was building up a case that would put a big dent in the Demons of Chaos Arizona chapters, and the Mother chapter, every now and then he would get some dirt on other chapters, during parties or at the clubs four mandatory national runs, when the whole club got together. There were other undercover ATF agents in the Demons of Chaos, but he was the only one to make it this far in Arizona, the stronghold for Demons of Chaos, he was under and alone.

Wild Bill was scared for his life the first six months in the club, always with the thought he'd be discovered and killed the way many Demons of Chaos enemies were out in the desert. ATF agents were forbidden to use drugs, but one night in a remote hotel during a drug deal he found himself in a bad situation.

The Demons of Chaos were buying drugs from the Mexican Mafia out of Southern California, when one of them thought he knew Wild Bill, and that Wild Bill was a Cop. He was Juan Caudillo and wild Bill knew him too. Juan was part of a sweep the ATF did against the Mexican Mafia on the RICO act. There was a standoff in that remote hotel out in the desert somewhere close to the border.

"What's wrong with your amigo?" said Chainsaw a member of the Demons of Chaos.

"He says your Brother may be a Cop."

"Is this some kind of joke" said Wild Bill, as all eyes were on him.

"No joke" said Juan.

"You prove you're not a cop" said the leader.

"First of all you spics don't tell Demons what to fucking do!" yelled Chainsaw.

Chainsaw pulled out his 45, within seconds everyone had their guns out, Wild Bill cut the silence that was thick with the promise of death.

"I ain't no fucking Cop" said Wild Bill "Are Cops allowed to use drugs?"

He went to the table were huge lines of speed were cut out, the kind only real hard-core users could do, Wild Bill grabbed the straw on the table and did the biggest line there. It felt like there was fire in his brain, his eyes started to water, and Wild Bill let out a "God damn!"

Everybody laughed and put away their guns. The Demons of Chaos walked out of the motel room with two pounds of speed, their lives, and Wild Bill with a new drug habit.

Wild Bill lost thirty pounds in three months and only slept two days a week. The Demons of Chaos somehow started to become his friends and his lifeline, and Wild Bill was becoming a real Demon. He had a new agenda, it was not

William Pike

to get caught by his own people, he still gave his reports and he was still piling up evidence, but mostly on Demons he didn't like, and today was one of those days.

Sin City chapter came to town and Wild Bill didn't like not one of the young punks, who thought they were better than the rest, and who didn't share their speed with Wild Bill, so it was time to make a report….

"Agent Becker."

"Hey its Jean in Arizona" said Wild Bill.

"Everything okay?" Asked agent Becker.

"Yeah fine, fine, the Sin City chapter is in town" said Wild Bill "They went to see Mother chapter, when they left the meeting they had their purple wings, rumor has it they earned them in San Diego this weekend. There's probably a dead woman somewhere out there with semen and saliva all over her."

"Interesting" said Beck "Where are they now?"

"Hell's kitchen celebrating."

"Okay I'll pass it along, you're doing a great job down there agent Jean."

The phone clicked and Wild Bill rolled a twenty dollar bill and did one of the four lines of speed off the mirror on his coffee table.

"See how you too cool punks like that!" Wild Bill said as the fire ate his brain, man he loved his job…

Chapter 28

"Peyton is one smart girl" said K0, as he looked at the pictures of the Nevada Chapter and the word Nevada written in blood on her forearm.

"Yeah she did good under the worst of circumstances" said Tommy "I'm very proud of her."

"What's our move now?" Asked KO.

"If I remember right, there's only three chapters of the Demons of Chaos in Nevada, Las Vegas, Carson City, and Reno. I say we start in Las Vegas and see if they like to rape little girls."

"We bringing Frank?" Asked K0.

"No, Frank has revenged his Daughter's murder, he can let her rest in peace, and move on with his life" said Tommy "I couldn't bring myself to tell him anyhow. I never saw someone enjoy a cold piece of pizza with a smile on his face before. I say we leave him be."

"Okay" answered KO.

"Head to my house KO, I got to pick up my cell phone and some clothes, we'll swing by your place and should be on the road by 11:00 PM.

When they got to Tommy's house, his answering machine was full with ninety nine messages, ninety eight of them were from friends of Peyton and Suzy's from school, all of them sending their love and support, and one was from Frank Simpson asking for Tommy to call A.S.A.P.

"Hello" answered Frank.

"Frank it's Tommy."

"Hey Bro" said Frank with a start.

Tommy smiled, Frank was one of the Brothers now, Tommy thought he earned it.

"Down at the gas station tonight, you know where the girls were… Were found, there was about three hundred to four hundred people there, all with flowers and cards, it was some show of love, I called because I wanted you to be able to see it."

"Sounds pretty amazing" said Tommy.

"It was indeed. Were having a viewing for Suzy Tuesday and then she's going to be cremated, after we want to have a memorial or reception party for the friends and family, I would love for you and KO to be there. I don't know where we'll find a place big enough, but I'll let you know tomorrow."

"We'll be there, and don't worry about looking for a place, you can use The Beach for the day."

After Tommy hung up he looked at KO.

"He called me Bro."

"Yeah, well I guess he is our Brother now" said KO.

"Hey call Cindy and tell her that we're going to be closed on Tuesday to the public. We're going to let Frank use it for Suzy's Memorial. Tell her to get together all the girls favorite music for the DJ and have it catered with Suzy's favorite food, for over four hundred people."

"Four hundred people?" Asked KO

"Yeah Frank said there was at least three hundred and fifty people at the gas station tonight, must've been some scene."

   Tommy and KO were in the yellow SS Camaro and on the way to Las Vegas by 11:00 PM. KO took the 15 north to the 215 back to the 15, within an hour and a half they were climbing the Cajon Pass, traffic was light and at 80 mph he thought they would be in town by 4:35 AM.

"Where we going to stay when they get there?" Asked KO.

"Not too sure Bro" said Tommy "Not too sure where were even going to start this hunt. I figure we'll find a popular spot that the locals hang out at, and see what we can learn about the Demons of Chaos, then we'll start stalking where ever they hang out till we can grab one of them."

They had just seen Barstow and were soon past the junction for I-40 and were once again on a long stretch of freeway cutting through the desert.

A car was coming up fast and KO could see its lights in the rearview mirror, he slowed to 70 mph in case it was a Cop, there was only a couple of cars on the road at 1:30 AM.

"What's up?" Asked Tommy.

"Car coming up fast, could be a Cop."

The car caught up within seconds, and slowed to match their pace at 70 mph. It was a black BMW 760i with nice wheels and blacked out windows. It speed away and then pulled back till they were next to each other again.

"I do believe you've been challenged to a race my friend" said Tommy as he buckled his seatbelt.

KO went from 6th gear to 4th gear and punched it, that SS Camaro jumped to a start, and the race was on, from 4th to 5th the super charged V8 screamed down the 15 like the beast it was, the BMW 760i kept the pace and KO shifted to 6th and in seconds they were doing 135, 140, the 760i stayed just a nose ahead of the Camaro.

"Jesus Christ whats that thing got in it?" KO yelled.

The Camaro topped out about 180 and wasn't going much faster when the driver of the 760i put the pedal to the metal and left the Camaro in the dust.

"Fuck me, they must be doing 210 mph or more" Said KO crushed.

He backed off the throttle and the BMW disappeared.

"Wow" said Tommy looking over at his very hurt looking friend.

"I got this car to make up for my Frank and Beans, now what am I going to do?" said KO.

It had been a while since Tommy really laughed, but he was laughing now.

They stopped in Baker California for gas, the world's biggest thermometer read 80° and it was 3:10 in the morning, it was starting to get hot in the desert and it was only late May.

They pulled into the Chevron and to their amazement, Tito the light heavyweight champion of the UFC was pumping gas into the black BMW 760i. When Tommy and KO got out of the Camaro, Tito looked over and smiled.

"Nice ride" said Tito with the same smile.

"Whatever" said KO still with his pride hurt.

"What's that fucking thing got in it?"

"Twin Turbo V12, tops out about hundred 190 mph to 220 mph" said Tito

"Holy shit, how much that thing go for?" Asked KO.

"About $150,000."

"Wow" said Tommy "Your Tito aren't you, the UFC fighter?"

"Yep" Tito said extending his hand.

"Tommy and this is KO."

"You guys fighters?" asked Tito.

"No were just bar owners" said Tommy "Headed to Vegas."

"Me too" said Tito as he put away the gas pump.

"Where's a good place to stay out there, if you wanted to hang out with local crowd?" asked Tommy.

"I'm staying at the Hard Rock Casino, it's just off the strip and it's always a good young upbeat crowd, a lot of locals party there also."

"When you fighting again?" asked KO peeling his eyes off the 760i.

"I got a third fight coming up in June with Chuck again."

"Well, we wish good luck to you, you're still my favorite" said Tommy.

They shook hands again and Tito pulled away in his 760i, while KO watched as if it was the first naked girl he ever saw.

They walked inside to pay for gas, KO went out to pump it while Tommy used the restroom, when he came out KO was sitting in the car.

"Hey you know the dealer you bought Peyton's BMW through?"

"Hank."

"Yeah Hank, you think he could give me a good deal on a 760i?"

"For the Frank and Beans?" Said Tommy.

"Yeah" said KO "For the Frank and Beans."

When they passed the State line from California to Nevada it was 4:08 AM, Buffalo Bills and Whiskey Pete's look like a ghost town, they drove right through and soon they saw the fabulous lights of Las Vegas City, the light of the Luxor was cutting up into the night sky.

"I say we get a room and get some rest, this town don't start rocking till later on" said Tommy.

"Where to, the Hard Rock?"

"Sounds good to me" answered Tommy.

They parked in the valet and Tito's 760i was parked in VIP parking, KO looked at it and shook his head. They entered the casino and right in front of them set two custom Harley Davidson motorcycles, Tommy took a closer look, one use to be to be Motley Crews and the other was owned by the Guns and Roses.

The casino was like a big circle with a big round bar in the middle, to their right was a club called wasted space, and even at 5:00 AM there were still a few people parting all around the casino. Tommy liked the feel of this place and wished he was there for other reasons.

They walked to the registration desk where a very sexy women was working behind the counter.

"How can I help you?"

Come to think of it every girl around was just about drop dead sexy.

"Two-bedroom suite please" said Tommy.

Her smile got bigger as she heard the word suite.

They took the elevator to the 19th floor and walked to room 1912, it was a nice room, with plush couches, chairs, flatscreen TV, and two connecting bedrooms, with their own bathrooms.

Tommy called for 2:00 PM wake-up call and went to bed.

KO was a little restless still thinking about the race with Tito, he opened the double doors and got an amazing view of the Hard Rocks pool, there were purple, pink, blue, and other colored lights shining off the Hard Rock and reflecting off the pool.

KO always wanted to come here, he wanted to go to that famous pool party the Hard Rock held on Sundays in the summer, it was called Rehab, they even had a reality TV show on E about it.

KO sat down on the plush purple velvet couch and grabbed the phone book, he would start his research right now...

"Hello."

Tommy answered the phone from a dead sleep.

"Two o'clock wake-up call" said a sweet voice.

"Thank you, I'm up."

Tommy rolled to a sitting position and called Peyton's room at the hospital, Justine answered on the first ring.

"Hello."

"Hi Angel" said Tommy "How you girls doing?"

"Just reading about this strange girl who loves vampires, it's a very odd story" said Justine "Peyton is recovering great the swelling is down a lot, and the Doctor says he'll be considering bringing her out of the coma in the next couple days."

"That's great" said Tommy "Thanks for being there Justine, you're a wonderful person and I love you."

"I love you Tommy, what's going on out there?"

"We are at the Hard Rock, I just got up, I need some food and then I'll get to work."

"Be safe baby, I want you to come home to us" said Justine "I've been having… Well, let's just say… I've been having very good dreams about you, the kind that we can make come true."

Tommy smiled.

"I'll be back late tonight or early tomorrow, if everything goes good."

"Be safe."

Tommy went to wake up KO when he entered the room KO was gone. Tommy went back to the sitting room and looked out the opened double doors that overlook the pool, there were hundreds of people out there and Tommy could hear the music all the way up to the 19th floor. In the bathroom he found a huge bathtub, he filled it up with hot water, got in and relaxed, trying to go over in his head what they needed to do, it was going to be a long day.

KO walked into the suite at 2:45, he seemed happier than Tommy had ever seen him.

"Were you down at the pool?" Asked Tommy.

"No" said KO walking to the still open doors "Damn there's a lot of trim down there" said KO.

"Trim?"

"Yeah trim, you know like ass" said KO "Speaking of trim and ass, you want to eat at the Pink Taco?"

"Pink Taco?" Asked Tommy.

"Yeah it's just outside the elevator it's Mexican food" said KO.

"I wonder if they really have pink tacos?"

William Pike

They entered the Pink Taco, it was a square area with a square bar in the middle, like everywhere else there was beautiful women working and a couple of guys with tattoos, this was Tommy's kind of place.

Tommy and his happy friend got a table. Lindsay their waitress, so her name tag said came to get their order.

"What can I get you guys?"

"I'll have the carne asada tacos with rice and beans" said Tommy.

"I'll take the same" said KO "And could I get a red bull and vodka also"

"Red bull and vodka?" said Tommy "At 3:00 PM?"

"It is Vegas" said the sexy Lindsay.

"Plus it's a great day" said KO.

"Maybe you should come here more often" said Tommy looking at his happy weird friend.

Lindsay left and then came back with KO's drink.

"Might as well bring me one too" said Tommy "It is Vegas right?"

"Right" said Lindsay as she walked oh so sexy back to the bar.

"I say we hit up the big round bar in the middle of the casino, find out where there's a couple biker bars" said Tommy.

"All right, there is a Harley dealer on Sahara" said KO.

"How do you know that?" asked Tommy.

"I saw it in the phone book."

They ate and drank, when they were done they left, on the way to the round bar they passed the poker room where Tommy could see Tito playing Texas hold 'em.

At the round bar they ordered two more red bull vodkas.

"You boys want to party?" said a sexy voice.

They were both tall, slim and were dressed in tight jeans, tube tops and five inch heels. Tommy was sure they were Hookers, KO just seemed to think he was still just having the best day of his life.

"Would you lovely ladies like a drink?" Asked Tommy.

He would use this opportunity to see what kind of information he could gain.

"I'm Sarah Beth and this is Lolo, we'd love a drink, but were only twenty and the Bartender knows us, how about we go up to your room and open a bottle."

Tommy looked at KO and Lolo was seated across to his lap.

"Fuck it, let's go" said KO.

They got to room 1912 and made their own red bull and vodka as Tommy pulled Sarah Beth to the side.

William Pike

"Are you girls working?"

"Yes, I thought you knew" said Sarah Beth.

"Oh I know, but my friend... Well, lets just say he thinks it's his lucky day or something."

Sarah Beth smiled, threw her long blonde hair over her shoulders and pulled her top down, they were two of the most perfect breast Tommy had ever saw.

"For three hundred dollars it could be your lucky day too" said Sarah Beth.

"You're very sexy, I mean very sexy" Tommy said "I'll pay for both of you, but tell Lolo... Not to let KO know she's... Working."

Sarah Beth smiled and Tommy paid her.

Back out in the sitting room, Sarah Beth took Lolo to the restroom. Lolo had full C breasts, long black hair to her ass, and dark blue eyes, she was a Vixen.

"What a day Tommy" said KO "I bet those two girls saw me pull up in valet today, and now they want to fuck."

Why would them seeing KO park in valet make them want to fuck? He wanted to ask but he let it go.

"What happens in Vegas stays in Vegas right" said Tommy.

"Fucking a right" said KO on his fifth red bull and vodka.

Sarah Beth came out of KO's room leaving Lolo behind.

"I think Lolo would like to see you KO."

KO got up, downed his drink and was off to see Lolo. Sarah Beth walked Slowly into Tommy's room while looking over his whole body with her eyes. Tommy got up and said the six hardest words he's ever had to say is life.

"Look I just want to talk."

After telling Sarah Beth about Peyton and Suzy leaving the Demons of Chaos out of it. Sara Beth told him about a couple spots for bikers.

An hour later Tommy and KO watched the girls walk out from behind, damn those six words. Tommy and KO looked out over the pool with a sixth red bull and vodka.

"Hey Bro thanks for paying" said KO "I just about wiped my bank account out today."

"You knew they were Hookers?" said Tommy "And how could you lose almost all your money?"

"I wouldn't say I lost it" KO said.

"I need to get you out of this city" said Tommy shaking his head "Let's go, I got the name of a couple bars we might find some bikers at, The Devils Pond and Hog Heaven"

"How did you manage that?" Asked KO.

"I'll never tell you, not as long as I live, what I had to do to get this info, no man, I mean no man could do it."

Out front KO handed his valet ticket to the Valet, smiling at Tommy the whole time.

"Quit looking at me like that." said Tommy "No more drinking for you."

The Valet ran to the car right next to Tito's 760i, what he got into was a 2010 dark midnight blue BMW 760i, he pulled out and stopped in front of Tommy and KO. KO tipped the Valet and Tommy got in, everything made sense now, the phonebook, KO being gone, the money, and that damn smile that was stuck on his face all day.

"Well, what do you think?" Asked KO.

"Your Frank and Beans must be feeling pretty damn good today" said Tommy "A car like this, a woman like Lolo."

"The Frank and Beans just got a whole lot bigger Buddy" said KO.

They went to The Devils Pond first, there was only two bikes out front. They went inside, it was a small place with two pool tables to the right and a bar to the left, they sat at the bar and ordered two Bud lights. There was only about six customers and the bikes must be the Bouncers or the Cooks in the back. It was only 5:00 PM.

"Any Demons of Chaos hang out around here?" Tommy asked the Bartender.

She had red hair, was maybe thirty, and not too bad looking. She looked at Tommy and KO's tattooed arms, and then looked around, the nearest customer was over at the pool table.

"Not around here, why are you asking?"

"I don't like to hang out where child rapists hangout that's all" said Tommy.

She nodded her approval.

"Then if I were you I wouldn't be going to Hog Heaven."

"I'll remember that thank you."

They finished their beers, Tommy left a hundred dollar tip and they drove over to Hog Heaven.

Tommy thought it was odd that the Demons of Chaos hung out at a place called Hog Heaven. The parking lot was dead and there was not a car or motorcycle insight.

"Better come back later KO, tonight sometime" Tommy said "Let's find a Home Depot or something, we need to get a couple things."

"I saw one off Tropicana" said KO.

The BMW 760i was a nice big car with lots of leg room, much nicer than the BMW 535 Tommy got Peyton, for $150,000 he could see why.

"When you think Tito will be leaving town?" Asked KO "I sure would like a rematch."

At the Home Depot they bought two ten foot lengths of chain, some duct tape and four locks. He knew Tommy always had a plan, so far they always worked, so KO didn't ask why. A volleyball court in a bar, who would've thought it would one day buy him a 760i.

When they got back to the Hard Rock, the Valet parked the 760i back in VIP and they went to their room.

Tommy switched on the flatscreen TV and turned it to the news.

"Last night at 12:21 PM David Kern hit the jackpot on the Megabucks and won $25 million" said the news lady.

Who was just as sexy as everyone else who worked out here.

"Wanted for the murder of a 24-year-old man in Arizona" she said as a photo of a man holding a gun which looked to be pointed at the camera "And the shooting of two others last night at a local Arizona bar Hells kitchen, anybody with information please call 1-800-crimestoppers."

They zoomed in on the photo, it was a man holding a 357, he was bald and had a vest on, on the right it said Demons of Chaos, under it Sin City, on the left he had white, brown, red, green, and purple wings.

"In other news, we're having a early heat wave...."

"Fucking Demons" said Tommy "They're everywhere."

"Seems like it" said KO "Wake me up when you're ready, Lolo drained me" and he went off to his room.

Chapter 29

Hog Heaven was on the northeast side of town, it was 10:00 PM and the place was busy. Inside there were about 40 to 50 people, older rough looking crowd, there were three Demons of Chaos that they could see, they all looked to be in their 40s, one walked by Tommy and KO's table, he was bald with a black and gray beard, his patch said Nevada on the back and in the front it said Las Vegas, he had a red cross on the right, so Tommy figured he must have killed for the club at one time.

Tommy and KO went and sat in the car and waited, it seemed like forever, and bars in Las Vegas stayed open 24 hours a day, but at 12:30 the bald Demon came outside. He walked past the bikes and got into a Ford F-150, it was white and look like it had never been washed.

"There goes one" said Tommy with a start "Follow him KO, but not too close."

They followed the bald Demon all the way to the southwest of Las Vegas close to some mountains, before long he pulled into an apartment complex, he parked in a spot and KO stopped behind his truck. Tommy got out with his 45 in his hand and walked up to the drivers window.

"Out of the truck tough guy" said Tommy.

"You know who the fuck you're fucking with?" Said the bald Demon.

"I sure hope so" said Tommy.

He pistol whipped the Demon across the face.

"Get out and get in the fucking 760i."

"Get in the what?" The Demon said confused.

"In the car stupid fuck!"

Tommy got in the back and duct tape that Demons hands behind his back.

"Tommy don't be getting blood on my new ride?" pleaded KO.

"Drive out towards the mountains" said Tommy.

"You going to tell me what this is about?" Said the Demon.

"Shut the fuck up! You'll get your chance to confess."

To confess? These guys are crazy! Were they on a mission for God or something? He kept his mouth shut.

"Turn right KO."

There was a construction site for new houses and they found an empty lot.

"Out" said Tommy.

He could see sweat rolling down the Demons bald head.

"Not so tough now are you, you fucking child murdering rapist."

"Rapist? What the fuck are you talking about?"

"Get out of the fucking car."

KO opened the back door and ripped the Demon out by his shirt collar.

"Take him over to that power pole."

Tommy grabbed the chains and four locks, when they got to the pole Tommy pistol whipped the Demon again and he fell. Tommy locked one end of the chain around the Demons left ankle and the other end around the pole.

"Back the 760 over here KO."

"The 760, why?" said KO worried about his new ride.

"Just do it, I promise no blood will get on it."

Tommy locked the other ten foot chain around the Demons right ankle, and when KO got the 760 into place he locked the other end to the undercarriage of the 760i.

"Hey what the fuck man!" yelled the Demon.

"KO pull forward till I say stop."

William Pike

The 760 rolled forward and pulled apart the Demons legs into the splits.

"Ahhh ... fuck!" screamed the Demon.

"Stop KO."

Tommy walked over to the window of the 760i.

"Okay Bro I'm going to ask this fuck some questions, he's going to answer or we'll split him in two, little by little. When I hold my hand up roll forward a little, when I put it down stop, if I give you a wave, pulled his piece of shit in two."

"Tommy, Bro… Where do you come up with this shit?"

"I learned a lot in prison" Tommy said with a smile.

Tommy walked back to the in pain Demon.

"My questions will be simple, answer them and you'll stay in one piece."

"Okay man, okay, I'll tell you anything."

"Friday night five Demons of Chaos raped two girls and killed one in San Diego, they were from Nevada, who are they?"

"Nobody from the Las Vegas chapter went to San Diego."

Tommy lifted his hand and the BMW rolled forward.

"Ahhh...Ahhh Fuck!" yelled the Demon, Tommy put his hand down.

"Last chance."

"Look man, look... There's two chapters in Las Vegas, there is the Las Vegas chapter and the Sin City chapter, there's five of them man, and they went to San Diego."

"Where are they at now?" asked Tommy.

"They have not made it back yet, they went to Arizona for some reason, fuck Ahhh.... I swear."

Tommy believed him and waved for KO to backup.

KO took off like he just started a new race with Tito, the Demon screamed as both legs ripped away from his body, leaving just the upper half, he tried to say something but died. KO got out and ran back to Tommy and the legless Demon.

"Looks like that hurt" said KO.

"I was waving for you to back up" said Tommy.

KO thought about what Tommy just said, and what he said to him in the car.

"You never gave me directions on when to back up, you just said if I wave split him in two, You waved."

"I guess I did" said Tommy.

They walked to the car and unlocked the right leg.

"It was the Sin City chapter, like the one on the news last night, there in Arizona."

"We going to Arizona then?" Asked KO getting back into the 760i.

"Not yet we got Suzy's Memorial to go to tomorrow" said Tommy "Let's go get checked out of the hotel."

"Think Tito's leaving tonight?" Said KO.

Chapter 30

Lugnut picked up his phone, the rest of the Sin City chapter was lounged around the Motel 6 just outside of Palm Springs California.

"Lugnut the cops got a picture of Skin, one of the victims had a camera" said Tom "They questioned everybody that was still at Hells Kitchen and they know he's riding with four other Demons, it might be wise for you guys to split up."

"Okay, hey sorry that went down at your place Tom" said Lugnut.

"Shit happens Brother, the other two victims are at the Phoenix hospital, last names are Rogers and Parker" said Tom "You want me to have someone make a visit?"

"That might be a good idea, a picture is one thing, but two eyewitnesses is another" answered Lugnut.

"Well, you Brothers keep your heads down and will clean up this on our end."

"Blood and honor" said Lugnut.

"Blood and honor."

Lugnut looked around the room and at Skin, he wanted to throw the phone upside his head.

"Hey smart guy" said Lugnut to Skin.

"Did you notice that those three guys had a fucking camera in their hands? They took a picture of you, and now the Cops got it."

"Ahhh man, what am I going to do?" said Skin.

"They also know there's five of us riding together, were not going to get very far if we don't split up."

"What's the plan?" Asked Romeo.

"We'll vote on what to do" said Lugnut "I say Skin takes off now, while they think were still in Arizona, cut west to the 15, get home, grab some shit, and go north to Carson City, till the heat cools down. Tom and the Phoenix chapter are going to take care of the two witnesses in the hospital, or we say forget it and stick together."

"No need to vote, I brought this heat on myself" said Skin "I'll take off."

"There we go then thats settled" said Lugnut "Call me when you get to Vegas and again when you get to Carson City."

They shook hands.

"Blood and honor."

Skin packed up and headed out the door.

Wild Bill was out of dope and money, this was a bad combination when you've been strung out for months. He looked at himself in the mirror, he had brown hair, but it looked black and greasy, his face was sucked up and he had black circles around his eyes.

"I need help" Wild Bill said to the mirror.

He wanted to get clean, didn't he?

"Yes" he said to himself.

Wild Bill walked to the phone and dialed ATF headquarters.

"Agent Becker" Wild Bill hung up.

"Fuck! Fuck! Fuck!" He yelled as he fell to the ground.

"I need help… Please!"

His phone rang, he thought for sure it was going to be Agent Becker.

"Hello."

"Wild Bill."

"Yeah."

"It's Tom, look we got a problem here that needs to be cleaned up, you want to be the cleaner? The pay is good."

Wild Bill sat up.

"Can I get half now and the other half after It's cleaned?" asked Wild Bill.

"I don't see a problem with that" said Tom.

"You at the Kitchen?"

"Yup."

Wild Bill was already putting his boots on, he found help, everything was going to be okay.

"I'll see you in twenty."

Chapter 31

Justine sat with Peyton and read most of the night, she gave Peyton another sponge bath, she thought she was looking really good for only three days, and the Doctor didn't seem worried.

Justine should have been able to sleep good, but Sgt. Nelson from the gang unit had called her, he didn't know she quit yet and he had told her information they received. The Demons of Chaos Sin City chapter was in Arizona and they were there to pick up their purple wings, which they earned in San Diego, Sgt. Nelson went through the details of how outlaw bikers get their brown, red, green, and purple wings. The Medical Examiner and the Lab tech reports all made a little more sense now, the two different traces of semen in each girl and the five different traces of saliva. How could she tell this information to Tommy? She couldn't… But she had to tell him about the Sin City chapter. It was 2:00 AM when she finally picked up the phone and call Tommy.

"Hey Angel, what are you doing up so late?" said Tommy.

"I couldn't sleep handsome" said Justine "Where you guys at?"

"We just left Las Vegas and are about to hit the state line, the way KO is driving we should be home in no time."

"He drive like a NASCAR driver in that yellow hot Rod?"

"You ever heard of a BMW 760i?" Tommy asked.

"I can't say I have."

"Well, it's KO's new Frank and Beans."

"Frank and Beans?" Justin asked confused.

That made Tommy laugh, just thinking about KO's Frank and Beans.

"Never mind."

"The reason I'm calling Tommy is, I found out some more info on the Demons of Chaos responsible for the girls."

"I'm listening."

"Well, from what I've been told it's the Sin City Nevada chapter, and there in Arizona."

"Yeah we found out the same info up here" said Tommy "And I saw on the news that they killed some guy out there."

"Really? I didn't hear about that."

"Yep, got a picture of the dumb ass and everything."

"I'm surprised you're headed home instead of Arizona."

"Suzy's Memorial is today, we'll be headed to Arizona sometime tonight, but I'll be in town long enough to make one of your dreams come true."

Justine smiled like she was still in high school.

"I might just hold you to that."

"I'm counting on it Angel."

Tommy hung up and thought about Justine's little haircut and her beautiful hazel eyes.

"KO, I thought this thing could do 190 or 220 mph" KO smiled and stepped on it, they were in Baker by 2:45 AM.

KO pulled into the same Chevron as they did on the way to Vegas, only this time he didn't pull behind a BMW 760i, he pulled behind a black Harley-Davidson soft tail, with Nevada plates. Tommy and KO didn't pay much attention to the bike, and walked inside, as the automatic sliding glass doors slid open to let them in a Demon stepped outside… The same Demon that was on the news. Tommy's heart skipped a beat, the Demon walked right by without a second glance. Once inside, they hurried and payed for gas.

"Five dollars on five please" said KO.

"You know that's only a gallon and a half" said the clerk.

"You must be a math major" said KO and walked out.

Tommy followed even though he had to pee real bad.

The Demon pumped his gas and walked back inside for his change.

"Can you believe this shit?" Tommy asked KO.

"Not really, what do we do?"

They got in the car and watched the Demon.

"We follow him till we get close to that exit ZZXXY, we smoke him and jump off the exit then back on the 15."

The Demon started his bike and pulled out, just as Tommy expected he took the 15 north.

"He must've ran from Arizona, not to close KO."

About five miles before the exit ZZXXY Tommy's heart was racing and KO was gripping the steering wheel with all his strength.

"Now ride his ass as close as you can, I want him to change lanes and let us by."

KO sped up and Tommy rolled his window down. At first the Demon just speed up, but the 760i stayed on his ass, they both pulled far away from the last car behind them and the Demon finally moved over to the right lane to let them pass, as they pulled up next to him the Demon flipped them the bird.

"Fuck you!" he yelled.

Tommy came out the window with this colt 45 and put seven rounds right in the Demons chest, he fell off the back of his bike and started tumbling hard.

"No fuck you!" Tommy yelled back.

The bike kept going and KO swerved away as it came into their lane, he almost sped right past their exit.

"Exit, exit!" Tommy yelled.

KO got off and then back on again, this time they stopped in Barstow for gas.

"One down" said Tommy.

"By my count that's eight" said KO.

"Well, one that….Well… Okay we'll call it eight."

Chapter 32

Homicide Detective Jimmy Johnson showed up at the Sheriff Department at 9:00 AM Tuesday and met his new partner Carl Spencer. Spencer was already in the office, he was young for a Detective at twenty eight, but was told he worked hard, JJ could already see that by all the reports spread out everywhere. Spencer stood up as he saw JJ coming.

"Detective Carl Spencer" he said putting out his hand.

"Jimmy Johnson, you can call me JJ."

"Jimmy Johnson, like our local NASCAR Boy."

"Yeah except I'm black and I drive a Chrysler."

Spencer laughed at JJ's only joke and he liked him already.

"So what do you think about this mess we got?" JJ asked.

"There's a lot going on here JJ, let me run what I think is going on by you."

"Okay shoot."

"Well, we've ID the group as Demons of Chaos, we got five different traces of DNA, but no matches in the DNA databank, so I'm guessing their young with no records. The San Diego chapter all get smoked one day after the crime and after we hear it's the Demons of Chaos, only it's not the San Diego chapter, as they all have records and we have their DNA on file, plus they were under surveillance all Friday night by our very own gang unit. San Diego gets smoked, then we get the pictures of the intersection and put it together with the Nevada on the girl's arm, there's four Nevada chapters, Las Vegas, Sin City, Carson City, and Reno. Then we get a break, the ATF says Sin City is in Arizona, and they got their purple wings, that they earned in San Diego, now we understand why there is so much DNA on the victims. So we narrow it down to Sin City chapter who's in Arizona, we know they're there because the ATF says so, and they killed one man and shot two other men in Phoenix. Meanwhile someone tortures and kills a Las Vegas chapter Demon last night in Vegas, we think around 1:00 AM, his body had no legs, one was locked to a chain and power pool, the other was locked to a chain about 50 feet away by tire tracks, I say they wanted to get information from that Demon. Then around 3:00 AM just outside of Baker a Sin City chapter Demons of Chaos gets shot off his bike on I-15 north bound. It's believed to be the same Demon that shot and killed the man in Arizona. I don't believe any of the Sin City chapter is in Arizona any longer, and I believe they've split up, which is going to make it hard on us to track the other four down. I know who did the crime and I know who they are, they're going down once we catch up to them. What I don't know is who's tracking down the same suspects and killing them, you got any ideas?"

This kid was good, real good JJ thought.

"Tommy guns Margolin and Brandon KO Smith" said JJ.

"Margolin the girl in the hospital's Father?" asked Spencer.

"The very same, Brandon KO Smith is his best friend, they've killed before and I believe they're killing again."

Chapter 33

Wild Bill was feeling a lot better, he had plenty of speed and money, yeah life was good. He took a shower, shaved, put on his black slacks, white long sleeve button up, black dress shoes, and black tie. He put his ATF badge in his pocket just in case he needed it. He looked in his mirror, yep, he was an ATF agent again, he rolled a hundred dollar bill and did a fat line of speed.

"Oh yeah…"

Wild Bill or Billy Jean grabbed two syringes, he was going to fill them with speed, but he didn't want to waste his precious dope, so instead he filled them both with drano, the pipe cleaner. He put the caps back on and grabbed his blazer jacket. He made it to Phoenix hospital by 9:00 AM. At the information desk there was an elderly man working who gave Wild Bill the room numbers for Rogers and Parker, 417 and 423. Wild Bill walked through the hospital and not one Nurse or Doctor gave him a second look. In room 417 there was a young man sleeping, he had been shot once in the chest piercing a lung, he had tubes in his chest and mouth, and an IV in his left arm. Wild Bill pulled one of the syringes out of his blazer and stuck it in the IV line and push the plunger down, the young man's eyes flew open and he half sat up and then fell back to the bed, he lay there with his eyes wide open dead. Wild Bill closed the young man's eyes.

"Rest in peace Mr. Parker"

When Wild Bill got to room 423 Mr. Rogers was awake, he had been shot twice, once in the leg and once in the stomach. He did have an IV but Wild Bill couldn't see how he would be able to put the syringe in it. Mr. Rogers was young, black, and looked at Wild Bill standing in the doorway.

"Can I help you?"

Wild Bill pulled out his badge.

"ATF, I just have a couple questions."

"I already talked to the Detectives."

"This will just take a minute."

With Mr. Rogers guard down, Wild Bill pulled out the syringe walked to the bed, with his right hand he slammed the syringe into Mr. Rogers chest aiming for his heart, he slammed the plunger down and Mr. Rogers gave a half scream and he was dead, with his eyes and mouth wide open.

Wild Bill left, as he walked by the Nurses station a nice
Nurse waved, of course being the good ATF Agent he was
he waved back.

Chapter 34

The viewing was a sad experience for Tommy, Suzy lay their dead, the happy smiling 17-year-old he grew to love. He knew Peyton was going to be crushed when she woke up.

Lisa Simpson was having a tough time, but Frank was holding it together, with his pride swelling as the hundreds of viewers shook his hand and paid their love and respect to his Daughter.

It was standing room only with many people waiting outside. The viewing lasted about an hour and a half and then they convoyed over to The Beach. The cars spread out for as long as the eye could see. At The Beach there were pictures of Suzy, Suzy with her Mom and Dad, Suzy with Peyton, Suzy with friends, Suzy with that beautiful smile, they were spread throughout The Beach on every table. Everybody brought roses and flowers, it smelled like a beautiful garden. The mood was somber at first then the DJ started to play Suzy's favorite music, people started to remember the good times.

Frank and Lisa showed up some 45 minutes later with Suzy's remains, the crowd quieted a little, Frank walked to the DJ booth, and grabbed the microphone.

"First of all I would like to thank all of you for the love and support you have shown Suzy, Lisa, and myself, it fills my heart with pride that Suzy touched so many lives. I know she's in heaven looking down at us all this very moment. I want to thank Tommy and KO for letting us host this memorial party here at The Beach, I only wish Peyton were here... With that being said I would like everyone to bow their heads in a silent prayer not only to Suzy but also to the beautiful Peyton on a full recovery and a happy life…"

Frank gave the crowd a moment as he wiped a tear off his cheek.

"Thank you, if everyone could grab a drink I would like to make a toast, if you're underage try not to let your parents see."

There was quiet laughter throughout the crowd, when it looked like everyone had a drink, Frank gave a toast, holding up his glass.

"To a beautiful life" said Frank.

"To a beautiful life!" everyone yelled.

"Okay DJ" said Frank "Put some of that Black Eyed Peas on, maybe my humps, I won't have my Daughter looking down from heaven saying great Dad way to ruin the party"

Everyone laughed and yelled for my humps and just like that there was a party, a party for Suzy's beautiful life.

The party lasted till about 10:00 PM Tuesday night, it would've went throughout the night if the kids wouldn't have had school the next day.

"That was some party" said Justine as she drove Tommy and Her back to Tommy's place.

"Yeah it was quite a sight" Tommy said.

He looked at Justine, taking in all her beauty, her short cute haircut showed her sexy neckline, her black dress fit tight to the curves of her body. He reached over and stroked her slender neck, she looked at him for a moment, just long enough to look into her beautiful hazel eyes.

"You're the most beautiful Angel" said Tommy.

Tommy led Justine through the front door and in the middle of the living room he turned and put his arms around her waist and kissed her long and deep, she held the sides of his face with both her hands as she moaned in his mouth. Tommy slid her dress off her shoulders one at a time and over her breast, then it fell to the floor, he pulled off his shirt. Justine ripped off his belt and his pants fell on the floor next to her dress, she pushed Tommy back and onto the couch. She stood in front of him and slowly took off her braw, letting him take in the view of her full C cup breast, she reached up and touched her erect nipples, she turned around and looked at Tommy over her shoulder as she slid her black G string panties off. Tommy was sitting there transfixed on Justine's beauty, she turned and straddled him on the couch taking him all the way inside her, she kissed him deep as she rocked her hips back and forth, slowly at first then a little faster till her whole body shook and trembled as she climaxed. She lifted herself off him and turned around one more time, she lowered herself back onto him, lifting herself up and down him in long slow strokes, Tommy grabbed her hips from behind, and Justine picked up the pace, faster, harder, until Tommy released himself deep inside her with a loud moan. Justine leaned back against his chest and kissed him over her shoulder.

"That was only one of the dreams I had" said Justine.

Chapter 35

It was 11:00 AM Wednesday, five days after the girls were attacked, Peyton was looking really good Tommy thought as he stroked her face.

"The Doctor says tomorrow is the big day Baby Girl" said Tommy "And soon, soon you'll be able to come home, I got a big present for you."

Tommy looked at Justine.

"Well, in fact I have two big surprises" he said with a smile "I love you Baby Girl, I have to leave again, but the Angel God sent us will be right here with you."

"You and KO be safe, I worry about you not coming back" said Justine "I wish you wouldn't go... I love you."

She looked at Peyton and knew he had to go.

"I love you too Angel."

"Why do you call me Angel?" asked Justine.

"Cause, I believe you are."

"Ready to go Bro?" said KO entering the room.

He walked over to Peyton and gave her a kiss on the forehead.

"Eight down Beautiful."

By 12:00 PM Tommy and KO were on the highway headed east for Phoenix Arizona.

"What's the plan?" asked KO.

"Same as last time, only we know where to start looking this time, Hells Kitchen."

"We need to get chains and locks again?" asked KO.

"No, I can't trust your lead foot" Tommy said with a smile.

"What... You fucking waved Bro" pleaded KO.

It was a beautiful sunny day as they drove to Phoenix, it took them six and a half hours to get to Hell's Kitchen and it seemed to be really busy for 6:30 PM.

Hells Kitchen Steakhouse and Nude Bar was set up just like a restaurant, only it had a huge stage in the middle, VIP room in the back, beautiful women walking around, bouncers here and there, and the best part of all to Tommy three Demons of Chaos sitting at a table.

"Bingo" said Tommy.

KO and Tommy got a table close by the Demons of Chaos and ordered steak dinners. To their surprise the dinner was really good, and there was a King like feeling watching beautiful nude women while you ate mouthwatering steak.

They soon learned that Hells Kitchen was owned by Tom a Demon and President of Phoenix chapter. He was tall and maybe fifty with gray hair. Tommy heard one of the girls ask a Demon if he would like a dance, she called him Wild Bill, Wild Bill refused and said he was leaving soon. Tommy and KO paid and went the 760i to wait.

Wild Bill came out with a small handbag, he strapped it to the back seat of his black Harley Davidson Road King and left. Tommy and KO followed Wild Bill to a three-story apartment complex, they watched from the street as Wild Bill unstrapped his bag and went up to the third floor. It was 8:15 PM and the sun was down, Tommy and KO followed.

"Grab the duct tape" said Tommy.

They took the stairs to the third floor and walked to the door Wild Bill went in, it was number 319. Tommy peeked inside the window, he could just make out Wild Bill, he seemed to be alone, and it looked like he was snorting a line of something. Tommy knocked on the door.

"Yeah" answered Wild Bill "who is it."

"It's Phil, Tom just sent me over from Hell's Kitchen" said Tommy.

The door cracked open, Tommy kicked it as hard as he could, it struck Wild Bill full on in the face. Tommy and KO entered, Wild Bill lay on the floor sleeping, on the table was a bunch of money and a Ziplock bag full of speed, maybe an ounce or more.

When Wild Bill woke up he was duct tape to one of his kitchen chairs, his legs were taped to each leg, his arms to the sides, with tape wrapped around his chest and chair, with a piece over his mouth. There were two men sitting on his couch, both with beers, they were big men with lots of tattoos. Who the fuck were these guys? Did they know who he was? The bigger one was counting Wild Bill's money and putting it back in the bag. The other one was loading a syringe with speed and water, way too much speed, he would kill himself if he did that much, then he looked up at Wild Bill, and Wild Bill knew it was for him not the man.

Tommy ripped the tape off Wild Bill's mouth.

"Ahh...What the fuck!" yelled Wild Bill "Who the fuck are you, you know who you're fucking robbing?"

"We aren't robbing you, you stupid fuck, we're about to ask you a couple questions, if you don't answer them, I'm going to stick this syringe in your left eyeball and fill it full of speed, I'm not sure what it will do, but I'm thinking it will hurt like hell and maybe blind you, then I'll ask again and move to the right eye" said Tommy.

William Pike

KO just sat on the couch drinking his beer, Tommy put the syringe closer to Wild Bills left eye.

"Okay, okay, what do you want to know man, Fuck!"

"Sin City chapter, where they at?" asked KO.

"They left, went to Palm Springs for bike week" said Wild Bill "They just came to town to pick up their purple wings."

Tommy's heart started to race, purple wings...

"What do you mean get their purple wings?"

"They earned them in San Diego last weekend, so they came to Arizona to get them."

"Who gave them these fucking purple wings?" yelled Tommy.

KO got off the couch. Wild Bill told them what they wanted but he felt like he was in even more danger than before.

"Mother chapter, the National President, Stomper man, it was Stomper... He's the only one who can give out awarded patches."

"Where does this Stomper live?" asked Tommy.

"I got a logbook man, in the bedroom closet with all the names and addresses."

KO went to the closet and came out with the logbook.

William Pike

"Why do you have all this information with dates and times?" asked KO.

After all Wild Bill's talking he was all of a sudden quiet. Tommy sensed something was amiss, he put the syringe as close as he could to Wild Bill's eye.

"Okay Fuck, I'm a cop... I'm fucking ATF."

KO looked at Tommy.

"Where's your ID" asked KO

"In the dresser, top drawer."

"What kind of ATF Agent does speed?" asked Tommy.

Wild Bill didn't answer. KO came out with a badge. Tommy put the tape back over Wild Bill's mouth and walked into the bedroom, KO followed.

"Holy shit!" said Tommy.

"What do we do?" asked KO

"We can't kill him he' a Cop, the ATF will be all over our asses, Demons of Chaos who rape and murder is one thing, but Cops, Cops will get everyone's attention" said Tommy.

"But he can ID us" said KO.

"We can't kill him... lets get the fuck out of here."

KO grabbed the money and Tommy took the ATF badge and the logbook.

Wild Bill set taped to the chair and was happy they left his speed.

1101 Desert view was a one-story house, it was tan and brown, with desert landscaping, it was a nice neighborhood and the streets were quiet at 10:00 PM. KO stayed in the car while Tommy got out with the 9 mm they got from Ken Smith a while back, the same one used on the San Diego Prospect. He held it just behind his back in his right hand and knocked on the door, it opened and a big man maybe three hundred pounds stood in the doorway, he had DFFD tattooed across the front of his throat in two inch letters, which Tommy thought stood for Demons forever forever Demons.

"You Stomper?" asked Tommy.

"Yeah who the fuck are you?"

Tommy answered with all seven bullets in the 9 mm and left the Mother chapter National President laying dead in his doorway. He wouldn't be giving out anymore fucking purple wings!

On the way out of town they stopped by Hells Kitchen one more time. When KO and Tommy walked inside there were four Demons of Chaos this time sitting at a table with the owner Tom. Tommy walked to the table and dropped the logbook and badge on it and left.

When Tom, Chainsaw, and Mikey got to Wild Bills the front door was cracked open. Tom pushed it the rest of the way and there was Wild Bill laying sideways duct taped to a chair.

Chainsaw set Wild Bill up and pulled the tape off his mouth.

"Thank God you Brothers showed up, I was just robbed by two Mother Fuckers."

"Did they rob you for this?" said Tom.

He threw the badge on Wild Bill's lap.

"Fuck... all right, all right, look Tom I work for the ATF, but I'm one of you guys now Bro, you're my family, my friends now... Didn't I just kill those two in the hospital?"

"Yeah I guess you did" said Tom.

"See Brother I'm one of you, I'm a Demon."

Mikey found an extension cord in the closet. Tom put the tape back on Wild Bill's mouth and walked to the sliding glass door that led to the third story balcony. Chainsaw tied one end of the cord around Wild Bill's neck, while Mikey tied the other end to the balcony railing. Then they both picked up one side of the chair and threw Wild Bill off the balcony, the cord snapped tight and broke Wild Bill's neck and left him swinging in the air. Tom picked up the bag of speed and they left.

Chapter 36

"Blood and honor" toasted Lugnut.

"Blood and honor" yelled the fourteen Demons of Chaos as they swallowed the shots of Jack.

Bike week had started and the main strip was alive with thousands of motorcycle riders of all types, sizes, and shapes, and along with that always comes the outlaws of the biker world and the Demons of Chaos Palm Springs and Sin City chapters picked The Old Saloon as their party spot for the night.

There was a good crowd and the bar had a mechanical bull, the crowd laughed as men and women were thrown off it. The Demons of Chaos bullied their way around the bar and the smart people moved out of the way, but every so often some unexpected biker would get slapped or punched. Once the Demons found their table the party started, shot after shot and line after line, the Demons of Chaos were alive and wild by 11:00 PM.

Rocky the President for Palm Springs had brought along a couple women who let all the brothers kiss and fondle them. They wanted to know when they would be asked to have a wing party? Stacy and Leah were turned on by the idea of being gang banged.

"Are you boys going to fuck and suck us tonight?" asked Leah.

She grabbed Turks Dick under the table.

"You'd like that wouldn't you?" said Turk.

"We both would" said Stacy.

"Wing party!" yelled Turk.

"Wing party!" yelled the Demons.

"Hey Lugnut you see that?" asked Romeo.

"See what?"

"There is a fucking Raider over there" answered Romeo.

"You fucking shitting me?"

Sure enough there was a Raider ordering a drink from the bar, across his back said Raiders on the top, a picture of a skull and cross bones in the middle, and California on the bottom. The Raiders where a rival biker gang and the last known to kill a Demon, they had been at war for over six years now. The last Demon they killed was Skip from Las Vegas chapter and he was Romeo's Uncle.

"He's mine" said Romeo.

"Wait… Wait till the time is right" said Lugnut "He don't see us yet, maybe he'll go to the restroom, then we'll make a move."

Lugnut's phone rang.

"Hello."

"Hey Bro it's Shovelhead" Shovelhead was a Demon from the Las Vegas chapter.

"What's going on Brother?" asked Lugnut.

"It's all bad up here Bro" said Shovelhead "Las Vegas Bruce was killed, and your boy Skin was shot off his bike on the 15 just outside of Baker, we think it might be the Raiders."

"Bruce and Skin… No fucking way!" said Lugnut "We'll leave for home tonight."

"I'm not done" said Shovelhead "San Diego chapters been wiped out, Stomper from Mother was shot down at his home, last but not least Wild Bill in Phoenix was an undercover ATF Agent."

"What the fuck is going on?" asked Lugnut.

He eyed all of his Brothers listening.

"We think the Raiders could be making a move, it's all we can come up with right now" said Shovelhead.

"Okay Brother will see you tomorrow."

"Be safe on the road, blood and honor."

"Blood and honor" said Lugnut.

"What was that all about?" asked Rocky "San Diego chapters all dead, Bruce from Vegas, Skin, both murdered, Stomper from Mother also murdered. Word is the Raiders are suspect, and there's one of those Mother Fucker's right there" said Lugnut.

All fourteen Demons of Chaos eyes burned into the Raider, it almost seemed like they willed him to go to the restroom. Romeo took off his patch so the Raider wouldn't get spooked, and he made his way to the bathroom. The rest of the Demons left to the street and started the bikes. Stacy and Leah jumped on back of Rocky and Chino's bikes from Palm Springs.

When Romeo walked in the Raider was using the urinal farthest to the left, there was maybe six men in the restroom, Romeo wanted his blood revenge and he didn't care how many saw the fuck get whacked. He pulled his five inch knife, walked right up behind the Raider and started stabbing him in the neck 1, 2, 3, 4, 5 times, blood was everywhere and the restroom was empty in seconds. Romeo wash his hands and walked out.

Chapter 37

Homicide Detective Jimmy Johnson slammed the phone down on his desk. Detective Spencer looked up from his report.

"Two more Demons of Chaos murdered" said JJ "The National President in Scottsdale, and get this an undercover ATF Agent posing as a Demon."

"This is getting serious JJ" said Spencer "We need to get Mr. Margolin and Mr. Smith off the streets."

"That's just the thing Spencer, I thought I had them nailed on this, the trail is following the crime and the Sin City chapter, but ATF says it was an inside job that killed their Agent, and they're pushing off the other killings on the Demons of Chaos rival the Raiders. I was about to tell him that's bull shit, but they got a dead Raider in Palm Springs and a dozen or more Demons of Chaos leaving the crime scene."

"But the DNA matches the I-15 victim" said Spencer "He raped the girls."

"Yeah it was the Sin City chapter, and we have enough for warrants now" said JJ "And I still think it's Tommy Margolin and Brandon KO Smith thats killing these Demons of Chaos, they're on the same trail as we are, and they're killing every Demon in their path, I bet my paycheck there in Palm Springs as we speak."

JJ picked up the phone and called Tommy Margolin's house, after four rings he got the answer machine.

"Not home" said JJ.

He dialed another number.

"Grossmont hospital."

"Room 312" asked JJ.

"One moments Sir" said the nice woman.

"Hello."

"Mr. Margolin please" asked JJ.

"Speaking" answered Tommy.

"...Hey Mr. Margolin... This is Detective Johnson."

"How are things coming along Detective?"

"Not much new... I was just calling to check on your Daughter's welfare, how's she doing?"

"She'll be awake today and on a speedy recovery I hope" said Tommy.

"I'm glad to hear that Mr. Margolin, thank you for your time."

"Who was that?" asked Justine.

"Your old partner, Detective Johnson."

"Really, what did he want?" asked Justine.

"Nothing, said he was just calling to check on Peyton."

"That doesn't sound like the JJ I know" said Justine "JJ doesn't get personally involved in cases, plus Suzy's his case not Peyton, somethings up. I have a feeling he's onto you, and was checking to see if you're in town."

"You may be right, he seemed surprised that I was here."

"Nope" said Detective Johnson "He's at the hospital."

"They'd have to drive all day and night with little sleep to pull off these killings in three different states" said Spencer "Maybe the ATF knows what they're talking about."

"Time will tell" said JJ "Write up those warrants and we'll get a judge to sign them."

JJ set back and stared at his map, somebody was on the Sin City chapters trail and Demons of Chaos were being killed at their every stop.

"You boys better pick up your pace" said JJ to himself
"Because I believe Tommy Guns and KO got themselves a
fast car and the noses of bloodhounds."

William Pike

Chapter 38

Peyton could feel and hear, this was new to her, she could only hear and think for so long, now she could feel the cold touch her skin, she moved her toe, it moved, it really moved… She tried to move her finger… It moved too… She opened her eyes, it was bright and hurt.

"There you go sweetheart, take your time" said a voice.

She opened her eyes again, there was a man… A Doctor with eyeglasses.

"Try not to talk or move your head, you're still in bad shape Sweetheart" said the Doctor.

She tried to open her mouth, she couldn't and the pain was great, the Doctor was right, she was in bad shape. Peyton looked to her right, her Daddy and a woman she was sure was the nice lady Justine who smelled like J-Lo, and uncle KO were all there smiling at her, Peyton smiled back, it hurt and a tear rolled down her face, but she held the smile for them. Her Daddy wiped the tear off her face.

William Pike

"I love you Baby Girl" said her Daddy.

Peyton said in sign language.

"I love you too" they all laughed, a Nurse gave her some water, it was the best water she ever tasted.

Uncle KO taught her sign language, he said he learned it in prison to talk from cell to cell without everyone hearing what they were saying. She signed again.

"Eight down?"

KO smiled and signed back "Nine down four to go."

She smiled her hurtful smile again and signed back.

"Nines good, please stop."

Peyton didn't want to lose her Daddy or KO, they're all she has. KO signed back.

"I'll tell him" and gave her a kiss.

"I love you" Peyton signed to her Daddy one more time and fell asleep like she had been up all night.

"Peyton wants us to stop hunting the Demons of Chaos" said KO.

"I know sign language" said Tommy.

Tommy got a Coke from the vending machine.

"But there are four left."

William Pike

"I'm sure she just don't want to lose us Bro, we're all she really has. She needs you and me in a bad way right now, we hurt those Demons bad, let the law finish it, I say let it go" said KO.

"By the way that Detective Johnson called me today, Justine thinks he's onto us" said Tommy "Okay we'll back off KO. Thank you for everything"

Chapter 39

Homicide Detective Johnson and Spencer faxed the warrants to Las Vegas Metro Police Department and within a hour they had ten uniformed Police Officers and a SWAT team around the Demons of Chaos Sin City chapter's clubhouse. It was a white building with red trim, with the Demons of Chaos patch painted on the wall, there were three motorcycles out front and a white Honda Civic.

The Spotter across the street, reported four moving bodies inside, three male, one female. Sgt. Baker was in command and he gave the order.

"Now, now, now!"

Tear gas was fired through the windows and they blew the door, the SWAT team was in the clubhouse and all the suspects were in custody in less than two minutes.

"Code 4, code four, clear" said Sgt. Baker.

"This Sgt. Baker, Detective Johnson please."

"This is Johnson."

"We served the warrants on the clubhouse, we got four in custody, three men all Demons of Chaos and one woman, two pounds of speed and nine guns. That's the good news, the bad news is that the Demons of Chaos are from the Las Vegas chapter not Sin City, they just share the clubhouse"

"You shitting me?"

"Sorry sir" said Baker.

"Good job guys, please send me a report" said JJ as he hung up.

"Not them" said JJ to Spencer.

"What now?"

"We wait" said JJ.

Chapter 40

Frank Simpson hung up the phone, his hands were shaking and his heart was racing, he sat there thinking through everything he was just told on the phone, he felt as if his Daughter was just killed again…

"Hello."

"Tommy?"

"Yep" answered Tommy.

"It's Frank… Frank Simpson…"

"Hey Bro… You okay?" asked Tommy.

Frank didn't sound right and he started to worry.

"Not really Tommy, I need to talk to you and KO, where you at?"

"We just left the hospital, KO was going to drop me off at home to shower before I go back to the hospital. You want us to stop by?" asked Tommy.

"No, I'll meet you at your house…"

Frank hung up, put his shoes on and headed out the door.

"Something's wrong with Frank" said Tommy.

"Like what" asked KO.

"Don't know, he said he needs to talk to us."

When KO pulled into Tommy's driveway Frank was already there waiting.

"Nice car" said Frank looking at the paper dealer license plates that said Las Vegas BMW.

"Thanks" said KO.

They all went into the living room.

"We killed the wrong Demons of Chaos" said Frank "Detective Johnson called me today, told me it was Sin City Demons of Chaos, and that they matched the DNA to one of them, but he was shot off his bike, and the other four seem to be on the run."

Tommy looked at KO and thought of how much he should tell Frank, but Frank kept Going.

"I think you two know this already, and I think you killed the one shot off his bike."

"Why do you think that?" asked Tommy

"The paper plates on the BMW say Las Vegas."

   Tommy went through the whole story from Las Vegas to Arizona and ended it with Peyton and the Detective being on their trail.

"Thanks for coming clean Tommy, and thanks for trying to keep it from me, you were right, my Daughter's murder just landed on me again."

"You going to be okay?" asked KO.

"I will be" said Frank "Right after I finish killing those fucks. I know you guys can't come, but I'll take over from here. I just need some help getting some guns maybe one of those pipe bombs" Frank said with his evil smile.

Chapter 41

Just outside of Palm Springs at the Marongo casino, Lugnut, Romeo, Turk, and Dave, sat at the main bar to have a toast to Skin, their Brother and Conrad.

"To Skin" Lugnut said "Blood and honor."

"Blood and honor!" yelled the Sin City chapter.

Other customers looked weary and tried not to make eye contact with the loud Demons of Chaos, security stood by at the ready as if any time they would start killing customers.

"I say we head to Los Angeles and hunt down some Raiders" suggested Romeo.

Who was still high on bloodlust.

"I second that" said Turk.

"We've been gone for days" said Lugnut "We need to get back to Vegas and take care of Skin, plus my Wife will be pissed by now. Speak of the devil, I swear this Bitch has ESP."

"Hey Babe" answer Lugnut.

"Where you at!" Said Shannon Lugnut's Wife of two years.

"On our way back to town."

"You might want to find somewhere else to go" said Shannon "The Cops were here looking for all of you, they have warrants from San Diego, they raided your guy's clubhouse and arrested some of your Brothers and one of your Whores there."

"When was all of this?" asked a sweating Lugnut.

"All this morning" said Shannon "Who was that Whore at the clubhouse Lugnut?"

"What, You stupid Bitch, is that all you care about?" yelled Lugnut "I'm three hundred miles away, who gives a fuck who she is" Lugnut hung up the phone.

"We got problems Brothers, Dave get a room."

Dave went to get a room and came back with a key.

"Room 256" said Dave.

Once in the room Lugnut broke the news.

"We all have warrants and the Cops are hunting for us, Shannon says there from San Diego, so this is real bad Brothers."

"Fuck what are we going to do?" asked Turk.

"I say we go to LA kill as many Raiders as we can and go out in a blaze of glory" said Romeo.

"This is real bad guys" put in Dave.

"We can go to LA like Romeo wants or we can go hide out at my Grandpa's old ranch, we could be safe there for a little while, we could let the heat cool down and then go to Canada or somewhere where we have other chapters" said Lugnut "Vote, all in favor of LA."

Only Romeo raised his hand.

"Three to one" said Lugnut "We go home to the ranch, we split up into twos and no flying our patches or colors, they'll be hitting every bike wearing red and white from here to Las Vegas."

"When do we leave?" asked Romeo.

"Me and Dave will leave tonight, You and Turk in the morning" said Lugnut.

The gang stayed in the room, ordered room service, and watched TV. At 10:00 PM Lugnut and Dave were getting ready to leave when the top story on the news was bike week and the murder of the Raider at The Old Saloon. The next story was about the raids in Las Vegas and then it showed four pictures, they were of Lugnut, Romeo, Dave, and Turk, it continued by saying they were wanted for the murder and rape of seventeen year old Suzy Simpson and the rape of Peyton Margolin, who was in stable condition at Grossmont hospital.

"Son of a bitch" yelled Lugnut "This shit just keeps piling up."

"Change of plans, Turk and I are going to San Diego" said Romeo.

"Fuck that!" Said Turk "I'm going underground."

"Well, I'm going Lugnut, we don't need no eyewitness" said Romeo.

"Okay Bro have it your way, I hope we see you at the ranch."

"Blood and honor" said Romeo.

They shook hands and hugged.

"Blood and honor."

Chapter 42

Tommy, KO, and Frank arrived at Ken Smiths house, who checked to make sure his Wife was out of ears reach.

"I put what you wanted in a duffel bag next to the garage. A 9 mm with silencer just like the last time, also a pipe bomb just like the last, and my very own favorite sniper rifle with a high-powered night vision scope, the Army is still looking for that baby, it's going to cost you."

"We got it covered" said KO.

He gave Ken the bag he got from Wild Bill in Phoenix.

"I'm worried about you guys, this shits been all over the news" said Ken "There has to be an end to this sometime."

"It will end when they're all dead" said Frank in a cold voice.

Frank walked out the door, grabbed the bag, got in his rented Ford Explorer and drove away.

"That guys a little uptight" said Ken.

"Imagine your Daughters been raped and murdered by five bikers just for the fun of it, just so they could get a patch to show others how sick and twisted they are, what would you do Ken?" said Tommy.

"I'd stick that pipe bomb up their asses" said Ken.

Frank was on the I-15 north bound, he was by himself and he knew he had to be smart or he might not make it home to Lisa and their soon to be born Baby. He thought his plan over in his head, simple is the best he thought. He had watched many movies and read tons of books, he wanted to go in shooting like Billy the Kid in young guns, like they did at the San Diego clubhouse, but he knew he would die, and Lisa needed him. No, he would do it like the movie sniper from far away without any return fire. He pictured it in his mind, one by one as they died, then he would feel at peace again...

Chapter 43

Justine gave Peyton another sponge bath, the Doctor still didn't want her out of bed, her broken jaw still made its so she was unable to talk. Justine didn't know sign language and today she showed up with a white marker board, it lit up Peyton's beautiful smile. Her first words she wrote to Justine were.

"My Daddy says you're an Angel, who got sent from God to look after us."

"God sent him to me first twenty years ago" said Justine.

Justine had grew to love this 17-year-old girl within days, it didn't take her long to figure out that Peyton was a very special girl.

"I wonder if all Angels smell like J-Lo" wrote Peyton as she laughed.

Justine smiled at this, and after Peyton's bath, she got her J-Lo perfume from her purse and sprayed some on Peyton.

Peyton seemed so happy for being in such bad shape and for being put through what she had been, maybe she was just happy to be alive.

"My Daddy loves you" she wrote.

Justine smiled yet again.

"And I love him" said Justine.

"I've never seen him love anybody but me and KO" wrote Peyton "I think I love you too."

Justine's heart swelled.

"I love you too Peyton, and all your words mean so much to me" said Justine "I'm going to do my best to fit into your lives, I hope this is okay with you."

Peyton smiled.

"I used to have a hair cut just like yours" Peyton wrote as she touched her head.

Justine could see Peyton's eyes starting to tear up, she tried to think of something funny to say, but came up empty. Instead she took the bathwater to the restroom and started to clean up.

She knew Peyton was trying to be strong for those around her, and that her scars ran deep, it would be a long time before she would be back to normal, if ever, Justine called out from the bathroom.

"Your Dad should be back with lunch soon, lucky you, you get yogurt and Jell-O again."

William Pike

Tommy had left to give the girls some privacy, he was a great caring man and she felt lucky to have him. Justine opened the bathroom door and stopped dead in her tracks, there was a man in Peyton's room, he had shoulder length hair, white shirt, jeans, and black boots. He was walking towards Peyton with a knife behind his back, Peyton's face had gone white, she looked scared to death. Justine's gun was in her bag next to the chair, she would never get to it in time, the man brought the knife out from behind his back. Justine didn't hesitate, she took five powerful quick steps towards the man and kicked his left knee as hard as he could.

"Ahh..Fuck!" he yelled out.

He went down, she tried to grab for his right hand and the knife but he was too quick and he stabbed at Justine, sticking her in the left shoulder twice, Justine threw herself back and tried to get to her bag, the man grabbed her ankle and she went down.

"Help somebody help!" yelled Justine.

The man stabbed her again in the back of the right leg, Justine kicked out and hit the man in the mouth, he fell back and she crawled in scrambled to her bag, she reached it as he caught her again this time stabbing her in the back, she could fill the knife blade hit her shoulder bone, she knew the death strike was coming.

"What's going on!" a Nurse yelled.

Justine flipped to her back with her gun in both hands now, a Glock 40, the man looked back from the yelling Nurse and Justine shot him in the forehead, blood and brains flew out of the back of his head and he fell back into a seated position, Justine knew he was dead but shot him two more times in the heart. The gunfire was loud in the hospital room, leaving your ears ringing, she could see the Nurse's mouth moving but couldn't hear the words. Justine's upper body fell back to the floor, she lay in a puddle full of her own blood, she felt weak, she looked over and up at Peyton in the bed, her marker board fell to the side, it said "Help!"

"Help" said Justine, and then she was gone....

Tommy got off the elevator on the third floor, he had a bag with lunch and two dozen roses, one for Peyton and one for his Angel.

"Bang!"

It sounded like a gunshot, it echoed down the hospital halls.

"Bang, Bang!"

He heard a Nurse scream, she was in the doorway of room 312. Tommy ran as other people did in the same direction to room 312, he came through the door holding lunch and roses, Justine lay on the ground in a great pool of blood, with Doctors and Nurses around her, a man lay up against the wall dead in his own puddle of blood, he was one of the Demons of Chaos he saw on the news, they called him Romeo. Nobody was trying to help Romeo, Tommy stood there helpless.

"Move Sir!" said a man with a rolling gurney.

Tommy moved and all the Doctors and Nurses picked his Angel up and threw her on the gurney and ran her out of the room, next to where her body lay was a white marker board, it said "Help!"

Tommy panned his eyes up, Peyton lay there staring at the dead Romeo, Tommy dropped the lunch and roses in Justine's life blood, he scooped up Peyton in both arms and took her from the room that smelled of death.

Chapter 44

Frank stayed the night in Las Vegas at the Hard Rock Hotel and Casino, Tommy said it had worked for him. He didn't sleep much, he lay there thinking what to do next, he knew that the Demons of Chaos he was looking for would be in hiding, the Cops were everywhere looking for them and their pictures were all over the news. Frank didn't have the look of Tommy and KO, he looked more like a Cop, every time he brought up Demons of Chaos people would get quiet or walk away. Frank went to the store at the Hard Rock, it sold everything from T-shirts to custom choppers. He bought himself some black jeans that cost two hundred and fifty dollars and a black T-shirt that said "Life's Short, Rock Hard" that cost fifty dollars.

Changing and feeling a little cooler he went back down for another shot, this time at the club Wasted Space. He had the same results, besides a light-skinned black girl who asked him if he wanted to party.

Frank retreated back to his room and lay there in his king-size bed.

"What am I doing here, I'm a car Salesman not a Detective."

Then it hit him, he was a car Salesman, he knew everything about his customers, his diehard Mustang clubs. He would start at a local Harley-Davidson dealership.

"Looking for a new bike today?" asked the friendly salesman whose name tag said Joe.

"I'm sure thinking about it" said Frank "But my Wife isn't too happy about it."

"I know the feeling, my Wife still gives me a hard time" said Joe.

"All of this biker business on the news isn't helping either" said Frank.

"Yeah it only takes a few bad apples to give us all a bad name" said Joe.

"What was their name... Oh yeah Demons of Chaos, don't they have a clubhouse around here?" asked Frank.

"Sure do, it's on the upper east side of town off Boulder Highway" said Joe "It just got raided by the police, I hope they close that place down!"

"Yeah that would be best for all of us real bikers" said Frank.

Frank walked to his rented Explorer and smiled to himself.

"Good job buddy" he said under his breath.

   He found the clubhouse without a problem, it was white with red trim all around except for the front door, it was bare wood and a construction worker was just finishing putting new locks on it. Frank waited and watched from just down the street. There was also a woman sitting in a white Nissan Maxima in front of the clubhouse, she had long blonde hair, but that's all Frank could see. When the construction worker finished she got out of the car. She was tall, had on short shorts and a white tank top, she paid the construction worker then she locked the clubhouses new door and drove away.

Frank followed the long blonde in the Nissan north up the I-95 they got off on Lake Mead and turned right. They were soon in an apartment complex. Frank thought this pretty long haired blonde girl must be important, after all she had the keys to the Demons of Chaos clubhouse. He parked and weighted, watching and hoping one of the four men would show up.

When Frank's cell phone ring he jumped.

"Shit!"

He picked up the phone.

"Hello."

"Frank it's Tommy."

"Hey Tommy."

"Look, those Demons might not be in Vegas" said Tommy "One showed up at the hospital and tried to kill Peyton."

"She okay?" Asked Frank worried.

"Yeah Justine killed the guy, but not after he stabbed her four times... I'm pretty sure she's dead, nobody will tell me anything."

"Okay Tommy... I think I'm onto something, I'm staying till they show their faces" said Frank.

It wasn't until 7:30 PM when the blonde left the house still wearing the same clothes. Frank followed her west on Lake Mead and over the I-95, she turned into a Smiths shopping center.

"Great" said Frank frustrated.

He parked and waited, she came out with a shopping cart, it had four bags and a 30 pack of Bud light in it. She went back down Lake Mead, but instead of going over I-95 she got on it northbound toward Reno. Frank's heart started to race and his palms got sweaty.

"Here we go" he said to himself.

She got off about fifteen minutes up the 95 and then headed west towards the mountains, there was only four cars heading west on this road. Frank drop back a ways, and soon it was only the two of them. She slowed and turned right on to a long dirt driveway and drove under a sign that read "Smokes Ranch" Frank kept driving when he looked over he saw three motorcycles.

"Bingo."

Chapter 45

Homicide Detectives Johnson and Spencer arrived at Grossmont hospitals third-floor about the same time as the Doctor.

"I'm Dr. Turner" he said to Tommy.

JJ and Spencer walked up and the Doctor stopped talking, he was older with gray hair and he gave JJ and Spencer a look of annoyance, JJ showed his badge.

"Homicide Detective Johnson."

"Very well" said Dr. Turner.

"There was a lot of bleeding and the loss of blood was great, she was stabbed through the leg and it cut a main artery, however we were able to stop the flow blood and Ms. Scott is alive, and should be fine, with a lot of rest mind you."

"That's great news" said Tommy.

"The dead man is still in room 312 Detectives."

Dr. Turner walked away.

"Ms. Scott" said JJ "Is he talking about Justine?"

"I'm afraid he is" said Tommy.

"Would you like to fill us in on why an ex-homicide Detective was in room 312?"

"She was saving Peyton's life" said Tommy.

He turned and walked back into 301 Peyton's new room.

"She's alive" said Tommy.

Peyton smiled and it didn't even hurt.

"Go give her a kiss silly!" She signed to her Daddy.

Tommy kissed Peyton and just about ran out of the room to recovery…

He got to Justine's room just as the Nurses were waking her up.

"Take it easy now Love, you've lost a lot of blood."

"Okay" said Justine in a whisper.

Tommy walked to the bed.

"I thought I lost you Angel" said Tommy holding her hand.

"You're going to have to do better than send one man with a knife to kill me off Mr." Justine said in slurred words.

Tommy laughed and kissed her softly.

"When I go I'm taking half" she said with a weak smile.

Tommy laughed again.

"Is that a wedding proposal?" Asked Tommy.

"Yes... How could you say no to a wounded woman in a hospital bed?"

"I Don't think I can Mrs. Margolin."

Tommy kissed her and stroked her hair, she was the most beautiful Angel he had ever seen.

"I Love you Angel."

"I love you Handsome."

Chapter 46

Frank parked just out of sight, his heart was pounding as the sky began to get darker. He grabbed his guns, pipe bomb, and ran toward Smoke Ranch at about fifty yards he hit the ground next to a huge boulder and took cover. He couldn't get his heart to slow down and he felt like he just got out of the shower, his shirt was soaked with sweat.

Frank lay down and trained his night vision scope on the ranch. It was old and unkept, with a barn off to the right about three hundred feet or so, there looked to be a stable to the left. Frank could see through the front windows of the ranch, it had no curtains or blinds only old wood shutters that were all open, through the left windows was a big living room, and through the windows to the right looked to be a bedroom.

The blonde went inside and two of the Demons of Chaos came out to get the bags of groceries and the Bud Light. Frank didn't have a clear shot, and he waited, just like the sniper in the movie, they would die soon, he knew, so he waited. He wished he could hear what they were saying, one of them left the room with the blonde, they reappeared in the bedroom to the right, Frank focused the scope on the Demon.

"Lugnut, I need to know, did you kill and rape a 17-year-old girl?" said Shannon Lugnut's Wife.

"What kind of stupid fucking question is that?" yelled Lugnut.

"I need to know the truth" said Shannon "I'm not going to be married to some sick rapist."

"You stupid Bitch, I'm only going to tell you this once, said Lugnut "Shut your fucking mouth!"

Shannon stood there staring at the man she used to love, before he was a Demon, before he was a murderer and a child rapist, she could see the purple wings, she knew what they were, she reached into her purse and came out with a small 22 caliber handgun.

"No, how about you shut the fuck up!" yelled Shannon.

She pointed the gun at Lugnut.

"You know I was raped as a little girl, how could you do that to a 17-year-old, use sick fuck?"

With the speed of a lightweight boxer Lugnut lashed out and punch Shannon in the nose.

"What the…" Frank watch the blonde pullout a small gun, but before she got a chance to shoot she was hit hard, she fell back onto the bed, he hit her again, then again. Frank wanted to shoot but he kept moving and hitting her, now she lay still on the bed and the man ripped her white tank top off exposing her large breasts, the man stood up and seemed to be undoing his belt, Frank had a shot and he took it.

"Boom!" the gun exploded like a cannon.

It shattered the window, and miss the man by inches, he jumped to the floor.

"Fuck! Fuck!" said Frank.

He trained his scope on the door of the bedroom thinking he would make a run for it. The door open but from the other side and a Demon stood there.

"Boom!" Frank's rifle screamed.

The bullet slammed into the chest of the newcomer, he flew back into the hallway. Frank Panned the scope over to the living room, nothing… Back to the bedroom, he only could see the half naked blonde, a flash of light caught Frank's eye to the left, a man was crawling out a side window. Frank set his sights on the left corner of the ranch house hoping he would poke his head out, It didn't take long, one of the Demons of Chaos looked and ducked back, he waited, while Frank waited, he looked again.

"Boom!"

The bullet it slammed into the man's forehead, the impact took him all the way off his feet.

William Pike

One of the motorcycle started.

"Fuck… fuck!"

Frank saw him coming from the side of the house.

"Boom."

The bullet slammed into the Demons forearm and he went down, he was in front of the house and slid behind the Nissan, Frank was up and running, when he reached the man he was sitting with his back to the car.

Lugnut was caught.

"Okay, okay I'm caught arrest me" said Lugnut "You fucking Pig!"

"I'm not a Cop" said Frank "I'm a Father."

He pulled out his 9 mm and shot Lugnut in the left knee.

"Ahhh fuck!" screamed Lugnut.

Frank shot him again in the right knee.

"How's that feel you sick fuck?" yelled Frank.

"I'm sorry man, I'm sorry" pleaded Lugnut.

"Sorry don't cut it" said Frank.

He shot Lugnut again in the shoulder. Frank heard noise behind him and spun around, it was the blonde half naked standing in front of the doorway, her left eye was swollen shut, her nose looked broken and there was blood all over her face and breasts as she stumbled forward. Frank could see her lips were split and a tooth was missing, she walked by Frank and kicked Lugnut in the knee, he fell to his side screaming.

"You fuck… You fucking Bitch!"

She kicked him again in the face, she stopped and looked at Frank.

"Finish him" said the blonde.

Frank pulled out the pipe bomb and stuffed it into Lugnut's pants only leaving the fuse out.

"I'm sorry, man I'm sorry" pleaded Lugnut.

Frank pulled out a lighter.

"Fuck I'm sorry…"

"Tell it to God when you meet him" said Shannon.

"Yeah" said Frank as he lit the fuse.

"God forgives, Daddies don't."

They jumped into the Nissan and sped away, the explosion went off as Frank got out of the Nissan at his rented Explorer, it shook the ground under his feet and sent a mushroom cloud into the sky hundreds of feet high. Frank reached into the Explorer and grabbed his white dress shirt, he threw it to the pretty blonde girl.

William Pike

"What's your name?" asked Frank.

"Shannon" said the blonde "Thank you Mr."

"You going to be okay?" asked Frank.

She didn't say yes but she smiled a bloody broken tooth smile.

"God forgives, Daddies don't... I like that" she said.

She drove away and Frank quickly did the same.

William Pike

Chapter 47

When KO, Tommy, and Justine turned into the Santana High School parking lot, KO picked the furthest empty spot to park his 760i.

"Don't what no damn kids dinging my doors" said KO.

It had been four weeks since Justine had shot down the outlaw Demon at the hospital, she was still sore but was recovering fine. Peyton was doing better than expected, her hair was a bout an inch and a half long, and besides the pain in her jaw she was doing great. She demanded to be allowed to go to her high school graduation, not only did she get to go, but Tommy threw her the keys to her new BMW.

"Hey have a look in the garage" Tommy said as she caught the keys.

Tommy had never seen her so happy. When Tommy, Justine, and KO got to the entrance to the auditorium Frank and Lisa Simpson were there waiting. Lisa was just about ready to have the baby, but she looked beautiful and Frank look like a proud man.

"Hey Brothers" said Frank.

They gave hugs all around.

"I had a dream last night that I got pregnant" Justine said to Lisa.

"Well, Tommy will just have to make that dream come true" said Lisa.

"Oh I gave it my best shot this morning" said Tommy.

Justine hit him in the arm and everybody laughed.

They found seats but the place was packed and there was excitement in the air. On the stage stood Santana High School's Principal, there were stairs leading up on the right and down on the left, which is the route the 2010 graduation class would take to receive their diplomas. The graduating class was seated in the front rows, they all wore purple and gold graduation hats and hats.

The Principal called their names one at a time in alphabetical order, when he reached and passed Peyton's name, Tommy started to worry that something was wrong. He could see Peyton though and she didn't seem worried, she sat in the very first seat in the front row.

"And last but not least" said the Principal "Peyton Margolin and Suzy Simpson."

The crowd exploded with cheers, one at a time they all stood up and yelled, whistled, and clapped their hands.

Peyton stepped up to the stage, once she was on top she thrust a picture of Suzy high over her head and the crowd boomed again even louder.

Tommy looked at Frank and Lisa they both had tears rolling down their faces.

Peyton walked to the Principal and received Suzy's and her diplomas, the crowd continued to stand and applaud the girl that had been left for dead, and her best friend Suzy, who was no doubt smiling down from heaven. Peyton stepped down from the stage and the whole senior class threw their hats in the air, a cheer went up again. Peyton walked past her seat and headed towards Frank, Lisa, Tommy, Justine, and KO, once she got to Frank and Lisa she stopped and handed them their Daughter's diploma, she gave them both a hug and they all cried one last time for Suzy, even Tommy and KO shed tears again, and they all joined in on the hug as camera flashes went off in the hundreds all around them and the class of 2010.

Chapter 48

"Beep, beep, beep, beep…"

Frank Simpson rolled over and turned off his alarm clock.
Like every morning it read 6:30 AM. Frank rolled back
over and spooned his Wife, he tickled her lower back
lightly with his fingers the way she loved to have it done.
He kissed her soft on the back of her neck.

Lisa would be having their new Baby soon, she was over
eight months pregnant, she still looks so beautiful to Frank.
He didn't know what he would do without her in his life.
Losing Suzy was the worst thing in the world, if it wasn't
for Lisa and the coming Baby he might've just ended his
own life. Instead he did what any rightful father would do,
he revenged his Daughters rape and murder. He rolled out
of bed and headed to the shower.

He thought about Suzy every morning as he walked down the hallway and saw her open bedroom door. The pain was going away little by little but it still hurt.

This morning as he walked down the hall he stopped and entered Suzy's room. Everything was just the way she had left it, even Peyton's backpack was still sitting on her bed. The only thing that changed was the picture and diploma Frank had hung up on the wall, just above her computer desk. It was the picture Peyton had carried at graduation and had given to him and Lisa. Peyton was a great kid and he loved her for all she had done, he had never felt so proud as he did when she walked across the stage and held his Daughter's picture high in the air.

He went to the kitchen and started his coffee, on the fridge was the note he had left for Suzy the morning she was missing, Every morning he told himself to take it down but he could never force himself to do it, he hoped maybe one day Lisa would while he was at work.

Frank walked out the door and headed to work, he got to his parking space and there sat his beauty, a 2010 Ford Mustang cobra, white with blue racing stripes.

Frank came home from Las Vegas to find his favorite car sitting in his place. Without a doubt he knew this was the Cobra from his work. When he walked into the condo Lisa looked up from the couch and smiled.

"How did that Cobra get here?"

"Well, I had to move the seat as far back as I could so my fat belly wouldn't hit the steering wheel and then I drove it all the way home like I stole it" Lisa said while she giggled "I bought it for you honey… Well, we both bought it for you."

"I don't know what to say Baby" said Frank.

"You're a great man, the best, life's short… and you only live once" said Lisa "You deserve the best."

Frank had secretly named his new car Suzy, and every morning it put a smile on his face. Maybe Lisa knew it would. He sat his coffee on the roof and unlocked the door, once inside he took a sip of his coffee. One of the neighbors walked by with a little dog of some sort. Frank turned the key to fire up that powerful supercharged V-8…

"Boom!"

The explosion was so massive it took out five cars to the left and right of the Cobra, it rocked the ground and complex, setting alarms off everywhere, the woman and her dog were thrown through the living room window of the nearest condo, thankfully she lived, the dog wasn't so lucky…

Chapter 49

When Homicide Detectives Johnson and Spencer got to the scene it was still blazing, the cars on fire were so hot you could feel the heat hundreds of feet away, the smoke was black and toxic.

Johnson and Spencer were called to the scene because one of the victims a Mary Stiller, who was almost blown up with the car, said there was a man in the first car that blew up, his name was Frank Simpson.

There were hundreds of people outside half dressed in robes and nightgowns, JJ spotted Lisa Simpson sitting on the front step of her condo, she was holding her stomach and rocking back and forth with tears running down her face.

"Ms. Simpson…" JJ said "Do you know what happened here?"

Lisa didn't say anything, she just kept holding her stomach and rocking, she was crying, but there was no sound coming from her, she just stared at her burning husband and held herself.

"Ms. Simpson?" JJ said again "We need to know what happened here."

Lisa gave out a painful cry, she grabs her stomach tighter and cried out again, water started running down the steps between her legs.

"Shit… She's in labor, get a medic Spencer!" yelled JJ.

Spencer ran for help.

"Just stay calm Ms. Simpson everything is going to be okay" JJ told her.

He held her hand and watched as the medics rushed over a stretcher.

"Call Justine please…" said Lisa.

"Justine… Justine Scott?" asked JJ.

"Yes… Please."

Lisa was rolled away and put in the ambulance. JJ had not talked to Justine since she was stabbed in the hospital, he had no idea what the fuck was going on! What he did know was someone had killed all the Demons of Chaos in the Sin City chapter and then some, now Frank Simpson was blown to shit, his Wife's in labor, and out of all the people in the world she could ask for him to call, she picked Justine…

It didn't take JJ too long to figure out why, when Justine showed up at the hospital, she was holding hands with Tommy Margolin and Peyton Margolin.

"How is she doing?" asked Justine.

"Don't know... Didn't really ask" said JJ "I'm here to talk to you."

Justine looked at JJ as if she never even knew him.

"Well, I think you might have picked a bad time" said Justine "My friends in labor and needs me right now."

She walked away and Peyton followed.

"Where's Frank?" asked Tommy.

"I was going to bring that up right before Justine bit my head off, Frank's dead, car bomb."

JJ watched Tommy, he closed his eyes for a minute, maybe deep in thought.

"Who did this?" asked Tommy.

"I think you know who did this Tommy Margolin" said JJ "Fathers aren't the only people who want revenge, I think you know that very well."

Tommy didn't comment, JJ knew a million things were flying around in his head.

"Look Mr. Margolin things could get real bad for you... and your family, you could be in great danger" said JJ "Help me out here, who do you think would want to kill Mr. Simpson?"

Chapter 50

The fire was beautiful, he watched it burn, he could feel the intense heat, even from this far away, it was hot, but not nearly as hot as the fire his Daddy would use to burn him when he was bad.

The explosion was incredible, the best he ever saw, his Son would've loved to see it, his poor Son.

"I'm sorry Boy, I should've been better to you."

He closed his eyes and tried to picture his Son, his last image was of an 11-year-old boy crying as his Daddy touched him.

The first time he had sexually abused his Son the boy was ten years old, he came home drunk one night and caught his son watching porn, porn that was taken out of his Father's closet, he had spanked his boy and then did other bad things to him. He knew it was wrong, he was sick in the head, he loved his boy and he even sent him to go live with his uncle in Las Vegas.

"I'm sorry Boy, Daddy loves you."

He popped open a Coke and watched the firefighters run around.

"I'll make it up to you Boy, one by one…"

William Pike

Chapter 51

"Frank's dead" said Tommy.

"Dead? What do you mean dead?" said a stunned KO.

"Someone blew his new car up this morning, with him inside it."

"Shit Tommy... This is bad" said KO "Demons of Chaos you think?"

"That would be my guess" said Tommy "But how would they know about Frank?"

KO watched his little girl and Wife swim and play in the pool, he took a quick drink of his cold beer then answered Tommy.

"I don't know Tommy, but we don't know what Frank did in Las Vegas or who he talked to."

"Yeah… I thought maybe they would come after Justine for killing the one in the hospital" said Tommy "But it's been five weeks and now this."

Tommy could hear KO's family in the background playing and screaming. He thought this was over… now Frank's dead.

"Lisa had the Baby" Tommy said "It's a girl, she named it Frankie Sue Simpson… This is all bad KO, we need to stop it before it gets worse."

"What are you thinking?" Asked KO.

"I'm thinking maybe the Iron Cowboys need to ride out to Arizona and call a meeting with the Demons of Chaos."

"I don't know Tommy, if they know we whacked Stomper, we could be walking to our deaths."

"If they knew that why hit Frank?" Said Tommy "I say we go see if we can stop this before it gets worse."

"Okay bro, you know I got your back" said KO "When we leaving?"

"I'm on my way home now, meet me there when you can."

Tommy hung up and walked back to Lisa's room, she was a mess, Tommy couldn't even imagine what she was going through, she had not even held her new baby yet.

"Justine" Tommy called out.

She came out of the room, Peyton was holding little Frankie Sue while Lisa was asleep.

"Hey Handsome" said Justine "What a morning."

"You're telling me... KO and I are going to Arizona to try to put an end to this, We're pretty sure who did this" said Tommy "But I don't think the Demons of Chaos know about KO and I."

"You could be wrong." said Justine.

"I know and I'm worried about you and Peyton, I want you guys to stay at a hotel till I get back to town."

"Okay Handsome, but you know I own a gun right?"

Tommy smiled.

"Yeah I know killer, but I got a feeling they are not going to show themselves" said Tommy "I should be back tomorrow sometime and I'll check in tonight when we get there."

   Tommy left a hospital with a lot of doubt in his mind, he hoped the Iron Cowboys past would help him call a truce with the Demons of Chaos... If not he would kill the new National President and then come back a few weeks later and try again...

Chapter 52

"This meeting is now in order" yelled Thumper, the Sargent of Arms for the Mother chapter of the Demons of Chaos.

"Brothers if you want to take the floor raise your hand, do not talk over another Brother, first violation is fifty dollars, every time after that is a hundred. This all members meeting has been called because of some issues that have come up with the Raiders... I'm turning the floor over to our National President Bumper."

"Blood and honor" yelled Bumper.

"Blood and honor" yelled close to seven hundred Demons of Chaos.

Bumper was 49 years old and has been a Demon for twenty years, it was his life and now he was at the top. He stood on the flatbed of a big truck in front of almost all of his Brothers, it was 1:00 PM July 3rd 2010, and he would never forget this feeling.

"First I want to thank all of you Brothers for making it here… We have some important things to vote on."

"The Raiders are begging for a truce… I think they've lost thirteen members now."

A yell went up from the crowd as they all cheered.

"Order!" yelled Bumper.

"You Brothers have done good, they started this war and were finishing it" said Bumper "I say we kill all the Bastards, but the good book says you all have the right to vote…"

Bumper gave them a moment to think, the crowd was quiet, this army of Demons was well disciplined, it gave him goosebumps to look out over all of them.

"A show of hands… All in favor of a truce" said Bumper.

Only about fifty hands went up. Bumper smiled.

"All in favor of death."

His army of Demon roared to life thrusting guns, knives, bats, and other weapons into the air.

"Death it is then!" yelled Bumper.

"You all know about the July 4th party tomorrow, we have guests coming and other clubs have been invited, show them respect…" said Bumper "We have some well deserved awards to give out. These awards are going out to the Brothers that put their neck and lives on the line, so you Brothers can wear those patches with pride, these are the Brothers that have the Raiders running scared. I love you all, but I love these Brothers a little more… If you don't like it get off your asses and put some work in… Phoenix chapter, Tom, Chainsaw, Mikey."

Bumper held up the three red crosses, the sea of red and white Demons of Chaos roared to life again as Tom, Chainsaw, and Mikey walked to the flatbed and got their red crosses for killing Wild Bill.

"Virginia chapter, Steve and Hank Junior…"

Chapter 53

He found her address in one week, Ms. Justine Scott. They had her name and picture in the San Diego Union Tribune, she had short dark hair, hazel eyes and a pretty smile. How could his boy let this girl kill him? Maybe his boy was less of a man for what his Daddy used to do to him. The newspaper treated her like a hero.

"Ex-cop saves 17-year-old victim."

It went on and on about how good she was and how sick his boy was. After he finished off her and her family, he would pay a little visit to the reporter.

He had sat out in front of her house for three weeks and nothing, she never came home, he would sit on the street and watch her house, he would think about all he was going to do to her, he would get hard thinking about Ms. Justine Scott, he stared at her picture in the paper and touched himself... He couldn't wait to get his hands on her.

Finally one day a dark blue BMW 760i pulled in, she jumped out of the back passenger door smiling, she ran into the house and was back out and in the car in less than sixty-seconds.

They drove off and he followed. How dare she be so happy! He followed the car to Santana high school, it parked and two men got out with her, big men, he followed them at a safe distance, they met a man and his pregnant wife, they all hugged… He watched them all cry and hug, it made him sick. He watched them during the graduation and how everybody cheered for the girl and the family, he made his mind up sitting there sick to his stomach, they would all die, every one of them.

Why wouldn't this Bitch come home? He decided to move to the next victim, the only other name he knew right now was Peyton Margolin.

He typed in the name in his handy-dandy laptop, on people finder .com.

"912 Second St. Santee, CA 92071" he read the information and he got hard again.

Chapter 54

Homicide Detectives Johnson and Spencer were back at the crime scene. The crowd was gone, only a couple of kids here and there trying to get a look. The Forensics Team was hard at work along with the Fire Department trying to figure out what was used for the bomb.

JJ and Spencer went door-to-door asking questions, did you see anything? Any strangers? Any bikers? Anybody messing with Mr. Simpson's car? They had been at it for two hours with no luck.

It was hot out in East County San Diego and JJ took a seat on someone's porch step, he thought about his old partner, he felt like he didn't even know her anymore. She did look happy though and he decided to be happy for her.

"You a Cop?" asked a kid on a skateboard.

"Sure am little man, you a Pro skater?" said JJ.

"Not yet" said the boy.

He was about twelve, he wore vans shoes, socks, and shorts, with no shirt, and his skateboard was a Tony Hawk.

"I think I might have seen the man who did this though."

JJ smiled his best smile.

"That's the best news I've heard all day" said JJ "Tell me what you saw."

"Well, last night I was skating in the parking lot, because it's summer and am allowed to stay out late" said the kid "I seen a bald man with a gray beard under Mr. Simpson's sick new car."

"What did he look like?" asked JJ.

"Well... I didn't get a real good look, I just know he's got a shaved head and a long gray beard... and this morning when my Dad sent me to the gas station to get a newspaper the same man was asleep inside a white van, I walked right in between the van and the car next to it."

"He was sleeping you say?" asked JJ.

"Yes sir, his eyes were closed and he had tattoos on his eyelids, the right one said game and the left one said over, game over" said the kid.

JJ got up with a start.

"Let's go have a talk with your Dad Little man" said JJ.

"Game over" said Spencer.

William Pike

"That's what he said" said JJ "Let's run it by the gang unit, ATF, FBI, anybody who has a record of having that tattoo, I want a profile on him A.S.A.P."

"I'm on it" said Spencer.

JJ needed to find this guy before he found his next victim. His thoughts were pulled away by his phone ringing.

"Detective Johnson."

"Hey Johnson its Deputy Stark, I'm on the Margolin house."

"Have you seen a bald man with a gray beard snooping around their?" asked JJ "That's what our suspect looks like, fifty to sixty, bald, graybeard, with game over tattooed on his eyelids, he's white and drives a white van."

"No sir nothing like that" said Deputy Stark "but two choppers just pulled out of Mr. Margolin's driveway, they had Iron Cowboy patches on... I've heard stories... and I don't think this is a good sign."

"You're right about that" said JJ "Keep your eye open and thanks for the call"

JJ hung up and made a call to the gang unit.

"Sgt. Nelson."

"Hey JJ what's up."

"The Iron Cowboys are back in town" said JJ.

"No shit... I thought one of my Deputies was going crazy" said Nelson "I just got a call five minutes ago saying two

Iron Cowboys were headed east on the I-8 freeway, they stopped following once they reached Alpine, looks like they're headed out of town, my guess would be Arizona, the Demons of Chaos are having a huge Fourth of July party."

"Son of a bitch" said JJ "Let's get them stopped, so they know we know what they're up to, and then warn Arizona."

"Yeah I would say there just might be some fireworks at this party" said Nelson.

Chapter 55

The 90° wind blasted against Tommy and KO's faces as they flew down and I-8 eastbound. Their custom choppers thundered down the highway.

Tommy loved the feel of his chopper underneath him, it usually made all of his worries and stress go away, but not today. Frank was dead, Lisa was alone with a baby now, and he was worried sick about Justine and Peyton. Would the Demons of Chaos really stop because Iron Cowboys asked them too? He didn't think it likely.

KO and Tommy stopped in El Centro and ate at Carl's Junior. It was hot out and they took their time, letting the sun creep down toward the West.

"Why do they call these Six Dollar Burgers, when they don't cost six dollars?" asked KO.

"You worry about the oddest things KO, we're about to go ask one of the biggest motorcycle gangs in the world to stop or else, after we just helped kill twelve of their members, and you want to know about the Six Dollar Burger."

"No point worrying about the future... I got a Six Dollar Burger in my hand right now" said KO.

Tommy look at his best friend and his Six dollar burger. Why did they call them Six Dollar Burgers?

Not more than three minutes after they were back on the I-8 east two California Highway Patrol cars were behind them. KO saw them first and then Tommy, they slow down to 70 mph and the CHP red lighted them.

"Fuck!" KO and Tommy yelled at the same time.

They pulled over and shut down their choppers, the sun was just setting and the to CHP's looked like silhouettes walking towards them.

"Good evening Boys" said a fifty or so man.

Boys? This was one of the good old country boys, sure enough he was chewing on a toothpick and everything.

"Good evening officers" said Tommy.

"Iron Cowboys huh?" said the good old boy "Where you Boys headed?"

"That would be our concern, not yours" said Tommy "If you got a reason for stopping us state it, if not we like to be on our way."

"Well, look it here Billy, we got ourselves a tough guy"
said the good old boy.

"There is an APB out on you two from San Diego, this is
just a friendly stop to let you Boys know that we know
you're headed to Arizona and Arizona be knowing it to, so
you just might want to turn and hightail it back to where
you came from."

"Well, thanks for the warning their Boss, but until we break
the law, how about you don't fuck with us" said Tommy in
a not so polite tone.

"Well, they're smart guy since you brought up the law,
Billy Boy here can fix you up with two speeding tickets,
it's 65 mph right here not 70."

The good old boy walked back to his car and no doubt he
was calling in their location, Billy Boy started their tickets.

"Nice talking slick" said KO.

"Fuck him" said Tommy "Boys… Do we look like fucking
Boys?"

Tommy and KO were back on the road and they were still
heading east, the sun was down and the air was cooler, it
felt good to get out on the road and put some miles on the
bikes.

KO was worried, he just like to not let it show. When they
pulled up to Hells Kitchen Steakhouse and Nude Bar, he

thought the whole world could see how worried he was. There were hundreds of Demons everywhere, they had huge tents set up in the parking lot, it was a sea of red and white.

"Holy shit!" said KO to himself.

Tommy couldn't believe his luck, he wished he would not have turned into the parking lot.

"Too late now" he said under his breath.

It seemed as if all eyes were on them as they parked their custom choppers near the front door.

"Well, nobody is shooting at us" said KO.

"I guess that's a positive" said Tommy.

When they got to the door, Tommy and KO were greeted like old friends.

"Welcome Iron Cowboys" said a young Demon "You know the party don't start till tomorrow right? But come on in there's plenty of good food and girls."

Tommy and KO got a table close to where they sat last time.

"What do we do now?" asked KO.

"Eat and then get the fuck out of here" said Tommy.

"Well, well, well Iron Cowboys" said Tom the owner of Hells Kitchen and President of the Phoenix chapter.

"I have not heard of the Iron Cowboys for some years now…"

Tom looked and waited for Tommy or KO to say something, when they didn't he went on.

"So you got any more ATF badges you want to let us know about? I guess we owe you one."

"No you don't" said Tommy.

"Well, everything is on the house tonight for the Iron Cowboys, even the women" said Tom.

He went on about business.

"Well, it's safe to say they don't know about us" said Tommy.

"Maybe Frank's car just blew up" said KO.

"I don't think so, but who knows."

They ate two steaks that were just as good as the last time they were there and they enjoyed the beautiful women dancing on the main stage.

"Maybe we should open a bar like this" said KO.

"Not in uptight San Diego, it would never happen."

An older Demon walked to their table with a smile on his face and an outreached hand, his shirt said "Fuck the Devils."

"Iron Cowboys, just wanted to pay my respects, I'm Crash."

They shook hands with the older Demon.

"Tommy Guns and this is KO."

"Where are you guys staying tonight?" asked Crash.

"Not sure yet" answered Tommy.

"Well, there is always room at my place, just say the word."

"We'll keep that in mind Crash, thank you" said Tommy.

"Seems like were mighty welcome here said KO" with a smirk on his face.

"Yeah I say we use it to our advantage" said Tommy.

Two sexy women came to the table.

"Would you boys like a dance?" said a long-legged bottle blonde with gold colored eyes.

"Not tonight Beautiful, maybe tomorrow" said Tommy.

She made a pouty face.

"I'm Goldie and this is Bobbi."

Bobbi had long black hair, both arms were covered with tattoos, she had big puppy dog brown eyes and she pouted too.

"I'm Tommy and this is KO."

"I'd really like to get on top of you in the back Tommy" said Goldie "I'll be looking for you tomorrow."

They watched the two sexy women walk away.

"Damn those girls were fine" said KO.

"Cowboys, my two best girls not good enough for you" asked Tom.

"No, there plenty good Tom, it's just that we're kind of on business" said Tommy.

"Business?"

"Yeah we were wondering maybe if you could set up a meeting with your National President."

"About what?" asked Tom.

"I'm afraid we can't say Tommy."

"Like I said we owe you one, I'll see what I can do, you guys come back during the party tomorrow" said Tom.

"We'll do that" said Tommy.

"Well, that wasn't too bad" said KO.

"Nope, maybe our luck has changed."

Chapter 56

Frankie Sue Simpson was the cutest little baby girl, she had blonde hair and blue eyes just like Suzy did, she weighed 7 pounds 11 oz. but felt much lighter in Justine's arms. She was all bundled up in a pink blanket and a little pink hat. The only time Lisa held her was to feed her. Poor Lisa, what was she going to do now… without Frank? She said all her family lived out in Iowa. Justine would be there for her.

"What time you got Peyton?" asked Justine.

Peyton looked at her new Fossil watch.

"8:10" Said Peyton.

"We better get going" said Justine "Your Dad went out of town for the night, that means we have our very first girls night out on the town" said Justine.

"Can we go Downtown?" asked Peyton.

"Sure maybe we'll stay at the W."

Justine and Tommy didn't tell Peyton about Frank... not yet anyway, she had just been through so much.

They drove to the house to get clothes for their night out in Peyton's new BMW. Peyton loved her new car, she volunteered to drive everywhere. On the way to the house Tommy called.

"Hey Angel."

"Hey Handsome, everything okay?" asked Justine.

"Pretty good so far, we got a room at the Hilton in Phoenix" said Tommy "We have been more than welcome out here by the Demons of Chaos, and I have a meeting set up for tomorrow, they don't seem to have a clue about us, I got a feeling someone else killed Frank, maybe he's done something in his past... who knows."

"Very interesting, I'll give JJ call and let him know, maybe he can dig something up" said Justine "Were still having a girls night out, we'll be at the W."

"Oh the W huh?" said Tommy joking "Be safe Angel, tell Peyton I love her."

Justine hung up and thought about calling JJ, but Peyton was right there, so she put it off.

When they turned onto Second Street there was a police car parked out front on the street. They drove by it and Deputy Stark waved. Peyton parked.

"Go pack something nice and sexy, I'm going to check on the Deputy out front."

"How sexy can I be with two inch hair?" said Peyton with a smile.

Justine walked to Stark's car.

"You my new bodyguard?" asked Justine.

"Something like that, how you doing?" said Stark.

"I'm happy… Considering all the drama."

"We just got a description of the suspect" said Stark.

"Really?"

"Fifty to sixty, white male, shaved head, long gray beard, tattoos on his eyelids that say game over, driving a white van."

"Well, that's good to know" said Justine "Any possible motives?"

"None that I know of, but people at the department seem worried about you" said Stark.

"Well, you be safe out here, we're going downtown for the night to the W."

"Okay I'll call it in, be safe" said Stark.

Justine called Tommy back.

"Miss me already?"

"Something like that, they got a description of the suspect in Frank's case, fifty to sixty, shaved head, long gray beard, white, with game over tattooed on his eyelids, and he's driving a white van."

"Okay got it, we'll keep our eye open out here, it seems like every Demon is in Phoenix for a Fourth of July party" said Tommy.

"Well, don't party too hard Handsome."

"I'll be good, just you don't be trying to sneak my little girl into any of those fancy clubs Downtown."

Justine laughed.

"Good night love."

    Deputy Stark watch Peyton and Justine pullout in the white BMW and not more than a minute later a white Ford van came down the street, the man driving was bald and had a graybeard.

"Fuck me!" said Stark.

The van passed Deputy Stark and was stopped at the light on Second and Magnolia, Deputy Stark flip a U-turn and hit his lights. The van pulled over to the right side of the road on Magnolia, Deputy Stark stayed in his car to radio for backup.

The back doors of the van flew open and the bald man was there holding some kind a rifle, Deputy Stark tried to duck but he was too late, the rifle was fully automatic and bullets ripped right through Stark's bulletproof vest, he was dead as the sixth bullet struck him, but the man fired 40 more rounds into the Sheriff car. He slammed his door shut and took off after his girly girls.

William Pike

Chapter 57

The front of Deputy Stark's car looked like Swiss cheese, 46 bullets ripped through the metal and glass. Deputy Stark was rushed to the hospital, but he was dead at the scene. JJ could see blood all over the inside of the car, empty shell casings from the AK-47 littered the ground. The scene just about put JJ over the edge, East County San Diego was becoming a war zone.

Witnesses described a white van being in front of the Deputy's car, but nobody saw the man. Deputy Stark had a dash camera and now JJ and Spencer drove back to the Sheriffs Department that had one Conrad less. Not one word was spoken from either Spencer or JJ, it was JJ's phone that broke the silence.

"Detective Johnson."

"Hey JJ, it's Sargent Nelson, we got a report from Phoenix, word is your boys showed up out there, it's said they been treated as guests, nothing hostile has happened, there now at the Hilton."

"What does that tell us?" Said JJ out loud.

"Ahh..I'm not sure" said Nelson "But there's over seven hundred Demons of Chaos out there, if they wanted them dead they would be."

"Frank Simpson is dead, now Deputy Stark is murdered just a half-mile from Tommy Margolin's while he was keeping eye on his house" said JJ.

"Somebody is after them that's for sure" said Nelson "But we don't think it's the Demons of Chaos, sorry to make your day worse."

"No, no... thanks for the update Nelson."

They got back to the department and you could hear a pin drop it was so quiet, the flag out front was already at half mast. JJ and Spencer went straight to the interview room equipped with a TV and DVD player, about fifteen Deputies followed.

The scene on the TV was unreal, it was like looking at a video game from the car view angle. Deputy Stark never had a chance... The back door of the Ford van flew open and the man opened fire, it killed the camera after five-seconds, but it was long enough to get a picture of the man and his license plate number.

Deputies just about ran out of the building to try and catch this cop killing madman.

"Run that plate number Spencer A.S.A.P!" ordered JJ.

"Mark Victor Lewis age fifty six, white male, brown hair, blue eyes, five foot nine inches, two hundred and thirty pounds. No criminal record, army vet of fifteen years, dishonorable discharge for sexual assault on POWs in Desert Storm. Last known address 1191 Canyon Dr. Lake Tahoe, CA 91923. Associate to the Demons of Chaos motorcycle gang…"

"Bingo" said JJ "Lewis is the same last name as the young man killed at Grossmont hospital by Detective Scott."

"I'll double check but I'm sure you're right" said Spencer.

JJ picked up his phone and called Justine.

"Hello."

"Hey little lady."

"Hey big guy any luck?" asked Justine.

"Some but it was not worth the price we had to pay to get it" said JJ "Deputy Stark was gunned down, just a half mile from Mr. Margolin's house…"

"No…" Justine gasped.

"I'm afraid so, 46 rounds from an AK-47, we have video from the dash cam, this guy is a madman and an ex Army soldier, he's also the Father of the Mr. Lewis you killed at the hospital."

That could've been Justine and Peyton on the side of the road… She stopped putting on her makeup and sat down.

"It don't take a genius to see he's after me and my friends" said Justine.

"That looks to be the skinny of it" answer JJ "Where you at now?"

"Downtown at the W, room 1224."

"I'm going to send a Deputy to sit out front" said JJ.

"I have Peyton with me also."

"Well, I think you'll be safe at the W, but I wouldn't leave, not for now anyway" JJ said.

"Okay, let me know when you get this creep!"

"Will do little lady."

"They found the van!" yelled Spencer through the door.

"Where at?" asked JJ.

"Hotel circle off the I-8" said Spencer "Also there is a report of a stolen rental car, a red Dodge Sebring from the same parking lot."

"This guy's not too smart" said JJ.

"No but he sure deadly."

Chapter 58

Tommy stepped out of the shower and dried off, his body still hurt from the long ride to Phoenix, when he walked into the living room of their two-bedroom suite KO was watching porn on the TV.

"You're like a six-foot three two hundred and seventy pound 15-year-old boy."

"What? I don't get to see the good stuff in my house" said KO.

Tommy was having trouble talking over the noise of the screaming women getting pounded, so he retreated to his room, just in time for Justine's call, he opened the phone walked to the door and threw it to KO.

"Phone" yelled Tommy.

KO pick the phone up, Justine could hear what sounded like sex.

"Oh...oh...yeah Big Daddy..."

Yep sex all right.

"Hello" said KO.

"KO."

"Ah....yeah."

"What are you watching?"

"....Harder yeah... like that... just like that."

KO turn the volume up instead of down.

"Yeah! Do it!... Do it! Fuck yeah!"

"Fucking remote" said KO as he tried to find the right button.

He threw the phone to Tommy as he laughed his ass off.

"Hello Angel" said Tommy between breaths.

"Hey Big Daddy... what are you guys up to?" said Justine.

"Oh fuck... my side hurts" said Tommy.

"They ID the killer, he's not a Demon, He's Mr. Lewis, a.k.a. Romeo's father, and he just killed the Deputy that was watching your house."

All of a sudden things were serious again and Tommy picked himself up off the ground.

"How do we find this guy?" asked Tommy.

"Every cop in San Diego is on it" said Justine "But I think it will happen soon, because he looks to be looking for us too."

"Stay at the hotel I'll be there by 12:00 tomorrow afternoon."

"Ride safe, they got a Deputy out front watching out for us" said Justine.

"Okay Angel, go ahead and give Peyton a heads up on what is going on."

"Okay Handsome I love you."

"I love you Angel."

Tommy sat on his bed and thought of what he could do to catch this guy. He heard KO turn the porn up a little loud.

"What the hell is that weirdo doing?"

After about four minutes he went to check. KO was nowhere in sight and the door to the hallway was wide open, the TV was extremely loud, Tommy found the remote and was going to turn it down when a young woman stepped into the doorway.

"Room service" she said.

She was holding a small plate with a bar of butter on it. She looked at the porn and then at the butter and smiled.

"You know there's complementary hand lotion in the bathroom right?"

Tommy got the TV turned down, now all he and the young room service lady could hear was KO laughing his ass off in his room.

Chapter 59

"Stupid fucking Cop! Just had to ruin everything didn't you?"

Mark Lewis was in a rage, he pushed the car's cigarette lighter in, once it was red-hot he pushed it against his forearm, he did it repeatedly till his rage started to go away. He missed his pretty white van.

"Oh, you girlies are going to pay!"

Mark lost the white BMW, he had such big big plans for the two lovely girlie girls… now he was stuck in an ugly red Dodge car, but he had his computer and he just loved all the stuff he could find on Google.

When he typed in Peyton Margolin's name all kinds of news popped up about her rape, and his son's death, and then even more Margolin stories… Tommy Margolin, Brandon Smith, Iron Cowboys, it just kept coming and coming. Now he had the whole little happy people circle right in the palm of his hand…

William Pike

"Time for the people finder.com" he said to himself happy as he could be in a piece of shit red Dodge.

"Brandon Smith... enter."

Mark Lewis drove by Brandon Smith's house three times it was just past 10:00 PM and the lights were on downstairs and upstairs, he parked and watch from across the street, he didn't see the big man named Brandon Smith, but he could see his lovely Wife and Daughter walking around.

"Oh..nice" said Mark Lewis while he touched himself.

They looked to be packing a couple bags.

"Where you going girlie girls?"

The Wife had sexy red hair, oh how he liked red hair. He got out of his car and creeped down the long driveway, he stopped by the detached garage and now got a better look at his prey.

"Oh Mommy you're looking good."

Mark Lewis pulled his old combat knife out and started around the back of the house. There was a nice pool and some chairs, the sliding glass door was open and he could hear his lovely girlie girls talking, his heart was beating fast and sweat rolled down his bald head, he stopped and listened.

"Why do we have to go?" said the girl.

"Your Dad didn't say but Justine and Peyton got us a room right next to theirs at the W" said the sexy redhead "It'll be fun."

"It's already after 10:00 PM I don't get it."

"Just pack young lady!" said Mommy.

The sweet Daughter went up the stairs and Mark Lewis made his move, he entered the house quiet as a mouse. He walked up right behind the sexy redhead, so close his erection touched her butt.

He hit her hard in the back of the head and neck, she fell face first into the couch and on her overnight bag, she was out cold. Up the stairs, he could hear his girlie girl to the right in her room.

He stood in her doorway and watched the sexy little teenager, she was on her hands and knees halfway into her closet.

"Mom, have you seen my black boots?" yelled the sexy bent over girlie girl.

"Do they look like these?" said Mark Lewis.

She screamed and jumped back onto her ass.

"Shh...shh...quiet now girlie girl" said Mark Lewis as he pointed the twelve inch combat knife at her.

"What... what do you want?" she asked.

He grabbed her by her hair and picked her up off the ground, using his knife he traced her perky little breasts and slid the knife down her sexy little body.

"I want you sexy girlie girl, but Mommies waiting on me, so you'll have to wait."

William Pike

"Please don't... why are you doing this?" she begged.

"Shh...quiet for now."

He laid her on the bed and tied her hands and feet with a telephone cord, he gagged her with a long tube sock.

She was wearing a jean skirt that now rode up onto her hips, he could see her little pink panties. He reached down and slid his finger into her panties and then inside her, she tried to wiggle away. Mark Lewis laughed and licked his two fingers.

"I'll be back" he said in his best Terminator voice.

When Gina came to she was naked and her arms were tied behind her back, she lay in the middle of the living room on the floor, she couldn't see anybody only several candles burning.

"Wakie wakie sexy red" said a cold voice.

A bald white man came into view, he was naked and had his hard penis in his right hand.

"If you scream your Daughter will die!"

Oh God Nikki my poor little girl. She just nodded, she could say nothing, in his left hand was a candle, he stepped over her and let it drip onto her nipples and breasts, it was so hot and burned but she didn't make a sound, semen dripped from the man's penis and landed on her stomach.

"Oops... sorry about that, let me clean that up" said the man.

William Pike

He got down on his hands and knees and licked his own semen off her stomach. This man was sick, Gina knew she was going to die. He sat up and spread her legs apart.

"I like it nice and shaved" said the sick and twisted man.

He dripped the candle wax on her vagina.

"I like it hot too" he said.

He put the candle out and shoved his penis inside her, she almost cried out but she held it back for Nikki.

Please God help us… He rolled her over and took her from behind. All she could think about was KO's colt 45 in his nightstand, she needed to get to it, she thought maybe he was going to come, but he stopped… God how long will this go on. He rolled her back over.

"No… I want you to taste it."

She pulled at her tied hands trying to loosen the knots, he raped her some more, she closed her eyes, he started to rape her faster and harder…

"Boom!"

There was a loud bang and she felt hot wet stuff all over her face and upper body, her ears were ringing. Gina opened her eyes the sick man was laying on his side with half his head missing, 16-year-old Nikki stood there with her Daddies colt 45 in both hands, she dropped the gun and ran to her Mom. Gina and Nikki looked at the dead man and almost at the same time they both read.

"Game Over."

William Pike

Epilogue

Gina and Nikki didn't tell KO our anybody but the police about the rape, they felt it best to leave that part out. But she did tell him she wanted to move, she couldn't live in that house anymore. Like Lisa, who refused to go back to her and Frank's condo, she stayed with Tommy, Justine, and Peyton. They decided to move also. All seven had been through a lot and felt they needed a new start in a new city. So they all picked up and moved. Leaving Cindy to look over the bar. They bought two houses on the same block, Tommy and KO opened a new bar, some say they went to Las Vegas, but nobody really knows, you can't even find them on Google or people finder.com.

Justine got pregnant and her and Tommy were married. Peyton started college and was trying to put the past behind her, she was going to counseling along with Gina and Nikki. Lisa filled her days with her new love, Frankie Sue.

All their lives had changed forever. For every action there is a reaction, which started as two 16-year-old girls

William Pike

sneaking out to buy a pack of smokes ended in seventeen people killed and families torn apart. Maybe if Tommy and KO had just watched their own special on HBO "Men who murder" they would've seen Manny Cole at the end. In prison for life for murdering the drunk driver who killed his 13-year-old son, which drove the drunk driver son to kill Manny Cole's whole family. Now he sat in prison for life with his whole family dead. HBO asked him one last question.

"Would you do the same thing again?"

Manny thought for a minute and with tears in his eyes he answered.

"God forgives, why couldn't I?"

Author's note

The characters, Motorcycle clubs, places, and story in this book are fiction, but the crime and ritual some outlaw motorcycle gangs practice and commit to earn white, red, green, and purple wings is real, down to every last detail.

William Pike

William Pike

44715771R00171

Made in the USA
San Bernardino, CA
21 July 2019